Missing the Midnight

Missing the Midnight

HAUNTINGS & GROTESQUES

JANE GARDAM

SINCLAIR-STEVENSON

First published 1997

1 3 5 7 9 10 8 6 4 2

© Jane Gardam 1997

Jane Gardam has asserted her right
under the Copyright, Designs and Patents Act 1988
to be identified as the author of this work

First published in the United Kingdom in 1997 by Sinclair-Stevenson
Random House, 20 Vauxhall Bridge Road, London SW1V 2SA

Random House Australia (Pty) Limited
20 Alfred Street, Milsons Point, Sydney,
New South Wales 2061, Australia

Random House New Zealand Limited
18 Poland Road, Glenfield,
Auckland 10, New Zealand

Random House South Africa (Pty) Limited
Endulini, 5A Jubilee Road, Parktown 2193, South Africa

Random House UK Limited Reg. No. 954009

A CIP catalogue record for this book is available from the British
Library

Papers used by Random House UK Limited are natural,
recyclable products made from wood grown in sustainable forests.
The manufacturing processes conform to the environmental
regulations of the country of origin.

ISBN 1-85619-673-9

Phototypeset by Intype London Ltd
Printed and bound in Great Britain
by Mackays of Chatham PLC

For William Mayne

Contents

Five Carols

Missing the Midnight

One Christmas Eve long ago, when I was twenty, I was sitting in the London train at York station, waiting for it to start. I was in a first-class carriage. I had been pushed into it. The rest of the train was packed. This compartment must have been unlocked at the last minute, like they sometimes do. Maybe it was because I had so much luggage. I was very glad to be alone. The compartment was sumptuous, with grey and pink velour seats and armrests and white cloths to rest your head against. I'd never travelled first class.

Just as the last doors were slamming, three people came into the compartment who looked as if they were there by right. They sat down two and one, the young man and the young woman side by side across from me, near the corridor, the old man on my side with the spare seat between us. I kept my face turned away from them but I could see them reflected in the window against the cold, black night. I had my hand up against my face.

I had my hand up against my face because I was weeping. The tears welled and welled. There had been no sign of tears when I was saying my bright goodbyes to the friend who was seeing me on to the train. I had waited to be alone. Now they rolled down my face and the front of my dismal mackintosh, and they would not stop.

I was leaving college a year early, having failed my exams and because the man I loved had told me the week before that he had found someone else. I was going home to my family, whom I despised and who had never liked me and were about to like me less. I had told them everything. Got it over in a letter. I hadn't yet told my mother, though, something which would cause her deeper distress – she was always in shallow distress – that I had also lately lost my faith. Anthropology had been my subject. I had just come to terms with the fact that it had destroyed my Christianity totally.

My Christianity had always been on a fragile footing on account of my mother's obsession with it. All she had seemed to be thinking about the previous night when I rang her was that if I was catching this late train I would miss the Midnight.

4

'But that means you'll be missing the Midnight,' she said. 'I'd have thought that the least you could do is come with me to the Midnight.' Then she said something nauseous and unforgivable to a daughter lost: '*All* the mothers will be there with their college daughters.' Oh my God.

All my mother ever thought about was what the neighbours might say, just as all my father ever thought about was how my achievements might improve his image at the bank, where he had been a desk clerk for most of his life. My father drank. He drank in the greenhouse at the end of our long, narrow garden in Watford. The greenhouse was packed with splendid tomato plants in summer and with heavy-headed old-English-sheepdog chrysan-themums in winter. Under its benches, all the year round, stood several pairs of wellingtons, and in every wellington stood a bottle. The bottles were never mentioned. They changed from full to empty to full again, invisibly. When my father came out of the greenhouse he would go upstairs to bed and cry. Then my mother would rest her head against the sitting-room mantelpiece and cry too. Then, as she also did after she and I had quarrelled, she would fling on her coat and dash to the church for comfort.

And she always came back much better. I would hear her feet tap-tapping briskly home along the pavement as I sat in my bedroom doing my homework. I used always to be doing my homework because I so wanted to get to college.

After the church visits my mother would sing to herself in the kitchen and start preparing a huge meal for my brother. She always felt forgiven after her prayers but she never came up to see me. Her life was my brother. He was my father's life too. He was supposed to be delicate and he had been long-awaited. When I was born, eight years before him, there had been a telegram from my father's family saying, 'Pity it isn't a boy.' My brother was in fact far from delicate. He was surly and uncommunicative and had the muscles of a carthorse. He detested me.

The only time I had been happy since my brother was born was the summer before, when I was in love. It was amazing how much happier my family had been then, too. Much more cheerful, and nicer to me. My mother had gone round saying, 'Esther's engaged to a graduate.'

There was another thing my mother didn't know, and neither did I at this time, and it was that I was harbouring a point-of-explosion appendix. I was thinking that the pain was anguish and my green face sorrow. Nobody ever looked as unattractive as I did that Christmas Eve. So I put my hand to my face and the tears rolled.

But I could not ignore my fellow passengers. The smell of them was so arresting – the smell of beautiful tweed clothes, shoe leather, pipe-smokers' best tobacco and some wonderful scent. There was a glow now in the compartment. Even in the glass there was a blur like a rosy sunset.

It was the young woman. She had stood up – we were on the move now – to go down the corridor. She drew back the glass door and slid it closed again outside, turning back and looking down through it at the young man. I felt for a handkerchief and took a quick glance.

She was the most lovely-looking girl in a glorious red coat. Her expensive hair was dark and silky, with shadows in it. Long pearls swung. Big pearl earrings. Huge, soft Italian bag. The hand that rested on the door latch outside wore a huge square diamond. Shiny red lipstick. She smiled down. He smiled up. They were enchanted with each other and enchanted because they felt their families were enchanted too.

I was astonished. There she stood. My mother always said that you should not be seen either entering or leaving a lavatory, yet here was this goddess, unhurried, waving her fingers at a man when she was on the way there.

The fiancé leaned comfortably back and smiled across at the man opposite, who could not be anybody but his father. He had the same lanky ease, though he was thinner and greyer and was wearing a dog-collar. This old priest now looked across at me, and smiled.

The trio seemed to me to be the most enviable human beings I had ever seen. It seemed impossible that anything could harm them: easy, worldly, confident, rich, blooming with health; failure, rejection, guilt, all unknown to them. And how they loved each other at this wonderful point in their lives!

When the girl came back they all smiled at one another all over again.

I could see that the girl did not belong quite to the same world as the priest. I knew she thought him just rather an old duck and that she had no notion of his job. I don't know how I knew this, but I did. And I saw that the son had moved some way into the girl's world, and would go farther into it. He'd got clear of all the church stuff. But nobody was worrying.

Was there a mother? Dead? What had she been? Cardigans and untidy hair and no time for anything? Or well-heeled, high-heeled bishop's daughter? Was there a sister? No, there was no sister. I knew the old man would have liked a daughter. You could tell that by the loving look he was giving the girl who was to become one to him.

Soon the fiancé fell asleep. Maybe we all fell asleep, for suddenly we were going through Peterborough and I was listening to a conversation taking shape between the girl and the priest, who, now virtually alone with her, was sounding rather shy.

'We shan't be in until after ten o'clock, I'm

afraid,' he said. 'Of course, it's much quicker than it used to be.'

'Oh, *much* quicker.'

'I suppose we'll be able to find a taxi. Christmas Eve. It may be rather difficult.'

'Oh yes, it may be *frightfully* difficult.'

'Andrew is very resourceful.'

'Oh, he's absolutely *marvellously* resourceful.'

'I'm afraid we shall miss the Midnight.'

'The Midnight?'

'The service. The midnight Christmas Eve service. Perhaps you don't go?'

'I'm afraid I don't usually—'

'D'you know, I don't blame you. I don't greatly enjoy it either, unless it's in the country. In London, people come crashing in from parties. The smell of alcohol at the altar rail can be quite overpowering.'

She looked bewildered.

'I should leave it till the morning if I were you,' he said. 'It's quieter. More serious people.'

Her red lips smiled. She said she would ask Andrew.

'I don't really care for Christmas Eve at all,' he said. He had removed his glasses to polish them.

His eyes looked weak, but were clear bright blue. 'Now, I don't know what you think, but I believe it must have been a very dark day for Our Lady.'

She wriggled inside the fuchsia coat and slowly began to blush. She lifted the diamond-hung hand to her hair.

'Think of it. Fully nine months pregnant on that road. Nazareth to Bethlehem. Winter weather. Well, we're now told it was in the spring. March. But it can be diabolical in the Mediterranean in March. I don't know if you've ever been to Galilee?'

The shiny lips said that they had never been to Galilee.

'Can be dreadful, I believe. And the birth beginning. Far from her mother. And the first child's always slow. Contractions probably started on the road. On foot or on a mule of some kind. One hopes there were some women about. And the birth itself in the stable. We're told it was an "annexe" now, but I prefer stable. Just think about it: blood in the straw . . . the afterbirth . . .'

He was unaware of her embarrassment.

She had no notion what to say. She was the colour of her coat. At last — 'We always have a family party actually on Christmas Eve. Absolutely lots of us. Terrific fun. I'm afraid we're not exactly churchgoers, any of us.'

'You will be having a church wedding, though?'

'Oh, golly, yes.'

'I'd very much like to marry you,' he said, lovingly, 'if that were possible.'

She looked startled. Then slowly it dawned. 'Oh – yes! Of course. Actually, I think Mummy has some sort of tame bishop, but I'm sure . . .'

'Perhaps I could assist?'

'Assist? Oh, yes – assist. Of course.'

He hadn't got there yet. The chasm was still just under the snow. He noticed me looking across at him and, at once and unselfconsciously, he smiled. I turned quickly away to the night, trying not to hear my mother's voice: 'I don't care what you say, Esther, there *is* a difference. Being a Christian does show.'

'You might just be interested in this,' I heard the priest say to the girl. He had brought out of his pocket a leather pouch, squarish, like a double spectacle case, and he leaned towards her, elbows on knees, and opened it.

She made a little movement forwards. Her hair brushed the fiancé's shoulder. 'How pretty. What is it?'

Had she expected jewels? A family necklace?

'What dear little bottles! Sweet little silver thing.'

'It's a pyx. A "viaticum", the whole thing's called. And something called an "oil stock". It's for taking the Sacrament to the sick in an emergency. I like to have it with me. It's an old-fashioned thing to do nowadays. It was a present from my parishioners. Very generous.'

She touched a little flask. 'Is it all right to touch?'

'Of course.'

'What are these?'

'Those are the oils. For Holy Unction. We anoint the dying.'

She jumped back. 'You mean – like the Egyptians? Embalming fluid?'

'No, just oils. Very ancient idea. Long pre-Christian, I dare say.' He knew that I was looking across again and he turned towards me and said, 'Wouldn't you, my dear?'

'Yes.'

How did he know me?

'It's for people on their last legs,' he said. 'Last gasp. *In extremis.*'

'Can it bring them back to life?' she asked. 'Is it sort of *magic?*'

'Well, yes. It has been known to restore life. We don't call it magic, but, yes – it has been known.'

He was looking at me.

When we reached King's Cross they were quick at gathering up their luggage. I took much longer to assemble mine, which was mostly in parcels spread about the overhead racks. My two great suitcases stood outside in the corridor. I had no money for a taxi and I wasn't at all sure how I was going to get all this to the Watford train. There might just possibly be a porter, but I had no money for the tip.

I let them go ahead of me, the girl first, still smiling, Andrew behind, touching her elbow, then the priest winding a long, soft woollen scarf round his neck. A present? From someone he loved? Someone who loved him?

I had no presents for anyone this year. Why should I? They wouldn't care. There'd be none for me, or maybe just a token. I didn't care, either.

Home in shame. A grim time coming. 'God help me,' I said automatically, in my heart.

The priest turned before he stepped out of the train. He smiled at me again. He still held the leather pouch. He lifted it in his hand in blessing.

They had all three disappeared by the time I got myself together and started to shamble after them down the platform. There was a tremendous queue for taxis, so Andrew must have been at his most resourceful.

I didn't need a taxi, though, or a train, or anything else. Both my parents and my brother were gathered at the platform gate.

The Zoo at Christmas

Christmas Eve, and twelve of the clock.
  'Now they are all on their knees,'
An elder said as we sat in a flock
  By the embers in hearthside ease.

We pictured the meek mild creatures where
  They dwelt in their strawy pen,
Nor did it occur to one of us there
  To doubt they were kneeling then.

So fair a fancy few would weave
  In these years! Yet, I feel,
If someone said on Christmas Eve,
  'Come; see the oxen kneel,

'In the lonely barton by yonder coomb
  Our childhood used to know,'
I should go with him in the gloom,
  Hoping it might be so.

The Oxen, Thomas Hardy

A pale, still day, the sky hanging white and low. It is the morning of Christmas Eve. The girl on the gate locks up at noon and waits around for the cleaner over in Refreshments. They go off together through the main gates, chatting down the lane to the pub. Over the other side of the Zoo, near Birds and Reptiles, the two resident keepers finish checking things and go off towards mince pies and a glass, the telly and the tree.

No human life stirs now within the Zoo. The toilets are locked; the kitchen of the cafeteria is washed down. Metallic, cold and colourless. The tigers look across. At it. Through it. Past it. Into the hoofstock enclosure. The tigers are fed on Tuesdays. Their weekly meal. This is Thursday. Not an urgent day. A flake or two of snow falls.

Word goes round. Electricity passes between cages without visible device. Ears can be switched on and off from within, out of boredom or pique or from the need for higher ruminations, particularly if we are talking tigers.

Tigers listen to other voices.

The feebler animals, the almost-humanoids, are always fussing to get through to the tigers. The

17

tigers don't notice them. They pace. They pace and pace, turning on their own tails, on their own dilemmas. Pace and pace.

Suddenly they speak. The Zoo listens. It is like Jove talking in the heavens. Whoever Jove is. The tigers stop pacing and listen to their own echo, flick the tongue. Yawn. Great sabres glisten. Then they flow lightly up the walkways kindly provided by the management, liquefy themselves along them, turn on to their long, striped, brush-stroked backs, raise their great paws, expose the loose material that hangs below the abdomen, silk and fluff, close their eyes. They ponder in their hearts the problem of the hoofstock.

The domestic hoofstock is recent. It consists of cattle, givers of milk and meat. Oxen and asses and silly great cows; farmyard creatures who have been introduced to the outskirts of the Zoo to familiarise children with the idea that all creatures are one. Ha!

The tigers drowse.

The less domestic hoofstock, the great bison, have been penned nearby, their mountainous necks like deformed oak trees. They look puzzled. Born in captivity, they have never roamed a plain, yet somehow they cannot feel that they are cows. 'They'll be giving kids rides on them next,' say the tigers. 'Look what happened to the elephants.'

Over in the sand paddock an elephant trumpets. Two Canadian wolves suddenly come trotting out of their den and stand listening. They run together up to the scrubby roof of the den and lift their noses. They start to howl, first one and then the other, like whales calling under the sea. Long, cold music. Something's afoot. Here and there throughout the Zoo, other messages pass. Lemurs, little black faces wrapped in granny swan's-down, let out bellows from unlikely lips. The great gibbons whoop. The strange snow leopard runs up and down its high platform on its big fur-soled bedroom slippers. It flings its wonderful misty tail around its neck like Marlene Dietrich.

'Who brought in hoofstock to unsettle us?' muse the tigers. 'Farmyard domestics. Thomas Hardy!'

For it is the new hoofstock who have put about this legend of Thomas Hardy's, that animals – particularly oxen, who are the elect – are wont to kneel before their Creator on Christmas Eve. They worship the Christ child. And sing.

'We do it, too,' says a Jacob's sheep. 'Several kinds of farm animals were present at the Nativity. We *should* worship.'

'I wasn't present at the Nativity,' says Ackroyd, the Siberian tiger. 'And Thomas Hardy was an agnostic.'

'Sing?' the other tigers say. '*Sing?*'

'We sing. We worship,' say the hoofstock.

'You don't catch me copying anything human,' says Ackroyd. Ackroyd is bitter. Ackroyd is not himself. He has not been himself for three months, since he ate his keeper.

The golden-lion tamarins, their black leather faces tiny as a baby's fist, scream and chatter at the idea of kneeling and singing, and worshipping their Creator, but they have been persuaded – oh, weeks ago – by the languid, pleasant cattle to give it a try. In fact, it is they who have organised the whole outing tonight, to the nearby church. They have done all the publicity. They have liaised with visiting squirrels and rabbits who know the neighbourhood. The venue is the farmer's field outside the Zoo; the time, 23.00 hours. A local sheep will lead them.

*

Escape from the Zoo will of course be no problem, for there is an excellent p.o.w. network of tunnels, always has been. The serval cats and bush-dogs make use of it regularly for night-time forages down the M2. The panther is scarcely ever at home. He went off as far as Canterbury the other day (Hallowe'en, the fool) and walked round the Cathedral during evensong. It was in the papers. He was compared to some tomcat on Exmoor. Washed his face in the sacristy.

'But that's panthers for you,' trembled the Zoo's one old lion (Theodore). 'They like humans. They feel affection.'

'Well, so does he,' said an elk, nodding at murderous Ackroyd. '*He* feels affection.'

Ackroyd looked baffled, but unrepentant. Tigers and penitence do not mingle.

'It's true,' called an elephant. 'Affection was what started it with that tiger. Up with his dinner-plate paws on the feller's shoulders. Lick, lick . . . Next thing, the keeper's in bits and Ackroyd's getting bashed with an iron spade, and then put in Solitary. I've seen cats do it with kittens.'

'Hit them with spades?'

'Don't be foolish. Licking. Love breeds violence; it's better avoided.'

'Only certain kinds of love,' said the yearning, ugly tapir with his anal-looking snout. 'Not worship.'

'*Worship*!' said the elephants among themselves. 'What do any of us know about worship? We're not lapdogs.'

'Just what *we* say,' fussed the Low-Church wallabies, the Quakerish giraffes, the pacifist bongos. 'What do any of us really know about love? But Thomas Hardy says that once a year, on Christmas Eve, we catch a glimmer. We are enabled to express our love to God and the Christ child. The experience is said to be agreeable.'

'God?' thinks Wallace, the gorilla, in the distance. He is the oldest inhabitant. He sits all day in the corner of his empire, the Great Gorillarium. He takes a straw from between his toes and holds it for an hour or two in his fist, pondering. His hand is the hand of an old farmer, purple, square-knuckled, with round grey nails. His domed, grizzled head is the shape of the helmet of the Black Prince. It is set between huge humped shoulders. Carefully he inserts the straw into the syrup bottle attached to the side of his cage, and sucks. He draws it out and re-examines it. Around him silly spider monkeys swing and spring. Two fluffy black baby gorillas, born last year, roll about covered in straw, the cage their world.

But Wallace can remember the rainforest. It returns to him in dreams; horizons beyond the diamond-shaped wire, vistas clear of hairless humans patched about with cloth. Winds and great rains. Scents of a river. Here, the snow is grey. Wallace in his thirty years has seen snow before. It does not excite him. Not as it does the snow leopard, who will now be up on his tree-shelf, purring. Bad luck for the public that it's not an open afternoon. They stand around for hours waiting to hear the snow leopard purr. Purring is his only sound.

Gorillas don't purr.

Pleasure? Happiness? Wallace's ancient eyes, the eyes that humans cannot face, the eyes that say, 'I am before The Fall. I am the one that knows' – Wallace's eyes ask: 'God? Christ?' Then, hours later, 'Worship?'

*

23

Yet he goes off with the rest. He accompanies them this night.

Nobody has expected him at all, but he turns up first. Timid antelopes, afraid of being late, come second. They are astounded to see his looming shape. They flicker off into the lane and stand between the farmer's hedge and the Canadian wolves, who, it being Christmas Eve, are uninterested in them. Next, the poor mangy lion, Theodore, comes creeping out of the escape tunnel and lies down with some local lambs. Red Kent cattle are standing about and the panther passes the time of night with them. The tamarins run about everywhere, flexing their tiny black hands, like tour guides with clipboards, and enigmatic langurs, like oriental restaurateurs on their night off, assist them. Where are the elephants?

'The tunnel's too small for them,' says a gibbon. 'They'll be kneeling at home.'

The giraffes?

'Yes. A giraffe has promised to be here. Vera, a nice creature. If her structure permits it.'

And, yes, here she is. Her delicate, knobbly, anxious little head emerges from the tunnel like a birth.

Monkeys galore follow her. It is 23.45. A quarter of an hour to go. '*Christmas Eve, and twelve of the clock*,' quotes an old ibex. '*Now they are all on their knees.*'

All is silent. Not a cold night. Snow settles lightly on the ground, on fur and hide. The snow leopard moves to a little distance on account of his rarity and distinction. He purrs. He sounds like a distant motorbike.

'This looks like the lot of us,' says the most human, the most mistrusted animal, the pied ruffed lemur, a donnish, dangly fellow once thought to be a form of Madagascan man who climbed trees in his pyjamas. 'Orl aboard, lads.'

But then there paced from the tunnel three tigers: Hilda, Enid — and Ackroyd himself.

Now St Francis, Easingbourne, is very close to the Zoo. Like many other old English churches built on pagan sites, it stands on a knoll. It is near the turn-off for the Channel Tunnel, down a wooded lane. Well before the Danes, things of a nasty nature went on here, and although a Christian presence was established in the sixth century the atmosphere is still not altogether settled. There is a sacrificial aroma. Two strange animal heads are carved on either side of the church porch. They're in Pevsner. Tall dark trees stand close.

For many years this church has been closed, but recent guidebooks have drawn attention to the beauty of the setting, especially in the spring when the knoll is covered with blossoming cherries, so that tonight, for the first time in ages, a celebration of the Midnight Mass is to take place, by candlelight. The approaching animals, who had banked on privacy, see the glow from coloured windows, hear the deep chords of an organ within.

'But it's *always* been empty,' fusses a sheep. '*Always* quite left to ourselves. Except for the angels. They arrive on the half-hour in the sky above. That's when we go into Latin.'

The three tigers stand apart, looking across the graveyard at the church with their terrible eyes. They lie down among the tombs.

One or two people are arriving – not many. They are walking up the path to the porch, passing under a bunch of mistletoe reminiscent of other times.

A woman with a small, muffled-up boy pauses beneath the mistletoe as she straightens him out; Terry Hogbin, thought to be retarded. He looks out over the graveyard and waves at a lynx. His mother pulls him into church.

'So we just wait here, then, do we?' asks a nervous bongo, most beautiful, most fleet of all antelopes, most aristocratic of hoofstock.

'I don't know. This isn't in the poem,' says a common sort of nilgai. 'Ask the bloody tamarins.'

The tamarins confer manically together. They can't say, they can't say. Stay or go?

The gorilla, Wallace, decides it. He sighs, raises his vast grey bottom and lopes on fingers and toes into church, where he sits in one of the empty pews at the back, a space before him and an aisle to his side. The rest, except for the tigers, follow without demur. The old lion Theodore snuffs about and settles by the shelves at the door, flat out, his chin in the hymn books.

The tigers sit out in the graveyard. Their sleek, ringed tails twitch once. Twice. Then first Hilda, followed by Enid, and at last Ackroyd get up and slide seamlessly in.

Melting snow from the pelts of the animals forms pools on the medieval flagstones. A smell arises, like fierce incense.

A parishioner sneezes.

The organ strikes up the first and most glorious Christmas hymn.

'Mum,' says Terry Hogbin, 'look at all them animals.' She says shut up and turn round.

But neither she nor Terry, nor any of them there, ever forgot the music of that night.

The parishioners said it was like a tape. There was a new vicar, a woman. They hadn't got to know her yet and she must have set something up. It was as good as the Bach Choir, they said, or the Nine Lessons and Carols at King's College Chapel. It was like angels.

And they talked of how the candlelight had shone in a most peculiar way. The crib with its holy family, surrounded by cardboard animals, had been bathed in a midnight sunshine. The baby in the hay had stretched out His arms towards a glorious world nobody there had ever suspected. It was a pity that Terry Hogbin had upset his mother by tugging at her sleeve and talking about giraffes.

And there was that stranger, an old hunchback, who came up after the Blessing to look in the crib. And made off. And the doll they had used for the Christ child had disappeared with him.

And, come to that, so had the woman priest. She'd stood out at the church door in the snow after the service saying happy Christmas to everyone, and good night, and nobody ever saw her again. Margaret Bean, her name was. A name with a ring to it, like it might be a martyr's.

And Ackroyd had gone missing, too, the tiger who had eaten his keeper. His tracks had not been among the others making their way home; tracks that were to amaze many people the next morning. Ackroyd wasn't caught until the day after Boxing Day, and in a very confused state. He remained confused, even desolate, ever afterwards. All his life. But tigers are funny.

As for old Wallace, he took the doll from the crib up to his private lodging in the cage top, and would sit staring at it, quite still, for hours. When the silly spider monkeys tried to get hold of it and snatch it about, he would show his might. He would rise up in his terrible strength and beat upon his

black, rock-hard breast, though (it has to be said)
he hadn't much of a notion why.

Old Filth

Old Filth had been a delightful man. The occasional kink, but a delightful man. A self-mocking man. The name had been his own invention, a joke against himself: a well-worn joke now but he had been the one to think of it first. 'Failed In London Try Hong Kong.' Good old legal joke.

He was Old Filth, QC, useful and dependable advocate, who would never have made judge in England. Never have made judge anywhere, come to that, for it was not what he had ever wanted. 'Failed' was his joke, for he had had exactly the career he had planned, to practise at the English Bar yet live as close to China as possible.

He'd been born in Shanghai more than eighty years ago, into a diplomatic family, brought up by adoring, bony Chinese amahs in slinky black dresses, tight buns of black hair scraped back into the nape of the neck. They had filled him with love and superstitions and the tangled forests of the fiery folk-tales he had loved. Old Filth spoke Mandarin and when he did you heard an unsuspected voice. All his life he had kept a regard for Chinese values, the courtesy, the hospitality, the respect for money, the decorum, the importance of food, the discretion, the cleverness. He had married a Scotswoman born in Peking. She was dumpy and tweedy, with broad shoulders, but she too spoke some Mandarin and liked Chinese ways. She had a Chinese passion for jewellery. Her strong, Scottish fingers rattled the trays of jade in the market, stirring the stones about like pebbles on a beach. 'When you do that,' Old Filth would say, 'your eyes are almond-shaped.' Poor old Betty, he often thought now. She had died after their retirement to Dorset.

And why ever Dorset? Nobody knew. Some tradition, perhaps. But if any pair of human beings had been born to be Hong Kong expats, members of the Cricket Club, the Jockey Club, stalwarts of the English lending library, props of St Andrew's Church, they were Filth and Betty. People, you'd say, who'd always be able to keep some servants, ever be happy hosts to any friend of a friend who was visiting the Colony. When you thought of Betty, you saw her at her round rosewood dining-table, looking about her to see if plates were empty, tinkling her little bell to summon the smiling girls in their household livery of identical cheongsams. Such perfectly international people, Old Filth and Betty. Ornaments to every one of the memorial services in St John's Cathedral that in the last years had been falling on them thick and fast.

Was it the thought of having to survive in Hong Kong on a pension, then? But the part of Dorset they had chosen was far from cheap, and surely Old Filth must have stashed away a packet? (Another of the reasons, he had always said so jollily, for not becoming a judge.) And they had no children. No responsibilities. No one to come home for.

Or was it – the most likely thing – 1997? Was it the unbearableness of being left behind to bow to the barbarians? The unknown Chinese who would not be feeding them sweets and telling them fairy tales? Neither of them was keen on the unknown. Already, some years before they left, English was not being spoken in shops and hotels so often or so well. Many faces had disappeared to London and Seattle and Toronto and rich people's children had vanished to

English boarding schools. Big houses on the Peak were in darkness behind steel grilles. At Betty's favourite jeweller, the little girls threading beads, who still appeared to be sixteen though she had known them twenty years, looked up more slowly now when she walked in. They still kept their fixed smiles, but found fewer good stones for her. Chinese women she knew had not the same difficulty.

So, suddenly, Old Filth and Betty were gone, gone for ever from the sky-high curtain-drops of glittering lights, gold and soft green and rose, from the busy waters of the harbour and the perpetual drama of every sort of boat – the junks and oil tankers and private yachts, and the ancient and com-forting dark-green Star-ferries that chugged back and forth to Kowloon all day and most of the night. 'This deck accommodates 319 passengers.' Filth had loved the certainty of the '19'.

They were gone, moved far from any friend, to a house deep in the Donheads on the Wiltshire–Dorset border, an old low stone house that could not be seen from its gate. A rough drive climbed up to it and out of sight. The house sat on a small plateau looking down over forests of every sort and colour of English tree. Far away, the horizon was a long scalpel line of milky chalk down, dappled with shadows drawn across it by the clouds above.

No place in the world could be less like Hong Kong. Yet it was not so remote that a doctor might start suggesting in a few years' time that it would be kind to the Social Services if they were to move nearer civilisation. There was a village half a mile up the hilly road that passed their gate; and half a mile in the other direction, also up a hill, for their drive ran down into a dip, was a church and a shop. There were other more modern, if invisible, houses in the trees. There was even a house next door, its gate alongside theirs, its drive curving upwards in the same way and disappearing, as did their own, out of sight. So they were secluded but not cut off.

And it worked. They made it work. Well, they were people who would see to it that the end of their lives worked. They changed. They discarded much. They went out and about very little. But they put their hearts into becoming content, safe behind the lock on their old-fashioned farmhouse door that could never be left accidentally on the latch. Old Filth gardened and read thrillers and biographies and worked now and then in his tool shed. He kept his QC's wig in its black-and-gold oval box on the hearth like a grey cat in a basket; then, as nobody but Betty was there to be amused, he moved it after a time to his wardrobe to lie with his black silk stockings and buckled shoes. Betty spent time sewing and looking out of the window at the trees. They went to the supermarket most weeks in their modest car and a woman came in four times a week to clean and cook and do the laundry. Betty said the legacy Hong Kong had left them was the inability to do their own washing. After Betty died, Old Filth took everything from her jewel box and sold it. He was leaving all his money to the Barristers' Benevolent Association, he said, because nobody felt much benevolence towards barristers. It was sad, really, that there was no one to appreciate the little joke. Nice man. Always had been.

It was the cleaning lady who destroyed it all.

One morning, letting herself in with her door key, talking even before she was over the threshold, 'Well,' she said, 'what about this, then? You never hear anything this place. Next door must have moved. There's removal vans all up and down the drive and loads of new stuff getting carried in. They say it's another lawyer from Singapore, like you.'

'Hong Kong,' said Old Filth, automatically and as usual.

'Hong Kong, then. They'll be wanting help but they're out of luck. I'm well suited here, you're not to worry. I'll find them someone. I've enough to do.'

A few days later Old Filth enquired if she'd heard anything more and was told, courtesy of the village shop, the new neighbour's name. It was indeed the name of another Hong Kong lawyer and it was the name of the only man in either his professional or private life that Old Filth had ever detested. The extraordinary effect this man had had upon him over thirty years ago and for many years after – and it had been much noticed and the usually cautious Filth had not cared – was like the venom that sprayed out from the mouths of the dragons in his old nanny's stories.

And the same had gone for Terry Veneering's opinion of Old Filth.

Nobody knew why. It was almost a chemical, a

physical thing. In Hong Kong, Old Filth, kind Old Filth, and swashbuckling Veneering did not 'have words', they spat poisons. They did not cross swords, they set about each other with scimitars. Old Filth believed that jumped-up Terry Veneering was all that was wrong with the English masters of the Colony – arrogant, blustering, loud, cynical, narrow and far too athletic. Without such as him, who knows? Veneering treated the Chinese as if they were invisible, flung himself into pompous rites of Empire, strutted at ceremonies, cringed before the Governor, drank too much. In court he was known for treating his opponent to spates of personal abuse. Once, in an interminable case against Old Filth, about a housing estate in the New Territories that had been built over a Chinese graveyard and had mysteriously refused to prosper, Veneering spent days sneering at primitive beliefs. Or so Old Filth said. What Veneering said about Old Filth he never enquired but there was a mutual, cold and seething dislike.

And somehow or other Veneering got away with everything. He bestrode the Colony like a colossus, booming on at parties about his excellence. During a state visit of royalty he was rumoured to have boasted about his boy at Eton. Later it was 'my boy at Cambridge', then 'my lad in the Guards'.

Betty loathed him, and Old Filth's first thought when he heard that Veneering had become his new neighbour was: 'Thank God Betty's gone.' His second thought was: 'I shall have to move.'

However, the next-door house was as invisible as Old Filth's; and its garden quite secret, behind a long stand of firs that grew broader and taller all the time. Even when leaves of other trees fell, there was no sight or sound of him. 'He's a widower living alone,' said the cleaning lady. 'His wife was a Chinese.' Old Filth remembered then that Veneering had married a Chinese woman. Strange to have forgotten. Why did the idea stir up such hatred again? He remembered the wife now, her downcast eyes and the curious chandelier earrings she wore. He remembered her at a racecourse in a bright-yellow silk dress, Veneering alongside — great, coarse, golden fellow, six foot two, with his strangled voice trying to sound public school.

Old Filth dozed off then with this picture before him, wondering at the clarity of an image thirty years old when what happened yesterday had receded into utter darkness. He was eighty-three now. Veneering must be almost eighty. Well, they could each keep their own corner. They need never meet.

Nor did they. The year went by, and the next one. A friend from Hong Kong called on Old Filth and said, 'I believe Terry Veneering lives somewhere down here, too. Do you ever come across him?'

'He's next door. No. Never.'

'Next door? My dear fellow——!'

'I'd like to have moved away.'

'But you mean you've never——?'

'No.'

'And he's made no . . . gesture?'

'Christopher, your memory is short.'

'Well, I knew you were—— You were both irrational in that direction, but——'

Old Filth walked his friend to the gate. Beside it stood Veneering's gate, overhung with ragged yews. A short length of drainpipe, to take a morning newspaper, was attached to Veneering's gate. It was identical to the one that had been attached to Old

Filth's gate for many years. 'He copied my drain-pipe,' said Old Filth. 'He never had an original notion.'

'I have half a mind to call.'

'Well, you needn't come and see me again if you do,' said courteous Old Filth.

Seated in his car the friend considered the mystery of the fixations that survive dotage and how wise he had been to stay in Hong Kong.

'You don't feel like a visit?' he asked out of the window. 'Why not come back for Christmas? It's not so much changed that there'll ever be anywhere else like it.'

But Old Filth said that he didn't stir at Christmas. Just a taxi to the White Hart at Salisbury for luncheon. Good place. Not too many paper hats and streamers.

'Hong Kong is still all streamers,' said the friend. 'I remember Betty with streamers tangled up in her gold chains.'

But Old Filth just thanked him and waved him off.

He thought of him again on Christmas morning,

waiting for the taxi to the White Hart, watching
from a window whose panes were almost blocked
with snow, snow that had been falling when he'd
opened his bedroom curtains five hours ago at seven
o'clock. Big, fast, determined flakes. They fell and
fell. They danced. They mesmerised. After a few
minutes you couldn't tell if they were going up or
down. Thinking of the road at the end of the drive,
the deep hollow there, he wondered if the taxi would
make it. At twelve-fifteen he thought he might ring
and ask, but waited until twelve-thirty as it seemed
tetchy to fuss. He discovered that the telephone was
not working.

'Ah,' he said, 'ha.'

There were mince pies and a ham shank. A good
bottle somewhere. He'd be all right. A pity, though.
Break with tradition.

He stood staring at the Christmas cards. Fewer
again this year. As for presents, nothing except one
from his cousin at Hainault. Always two handker-
chiefs. Well, more than he ever sent her. He must
remember to send some flowers or something. He
picked up a large, glossy card and read: 'A Merry
Christmas from The Ideal Tailor, Century Arcade,

Star Building, to our esteemed client.' Every year. Never failed. Still had his suits. Twenty years old. Snowflakes danced around a Chinese house on stilts. Red Chinese characters and a rosy Father Christmas in the corner.

Suddenly he missed Betty. Longed for Betty. Felt that if he turned round quickly, there she would be.

But she was not.

Outside there was a strange sound, a long sliding noise and a thump. A heavy thump. It might well be the taxi skidding on the drive and hitting the house. Filth opened the front door and saw nothing but snow. He stepped quickly out on to his doorstep for a moment, to look down the drive, and the front door swung to behind him, fastening with a solid, pre-war click.

He was in bedroom slippers. Otherwise he was wearing trousers, a singlet – which he always wore, being a gentleman, thank God – shirt and tie and a thin cashmere cardigan Betty had bought him years ago. It was already sopped through.

Filth walked delicately round the outside of the house, bent forward, screwing up his eyes against the snow, to see if by any chance . . . but he knew

43

that the back door was locked and all the windows. He turned off towards the toolshed, over the invisible slippery grass. Locked. He thought of the car in the garage. He hadn't driven it for some time. Mrs Thing did the shopping now. It was scarcely used. But maybe the garage?

The garage was locked.

Nothing for it but to get down the drive somehow and wait for the taxi under Veneering's yews.

On his tiptoe way he passed the heap of snow that had fallen off the roof and sounded like a slithering car. 'I'm a bloody old fool,' said Filth.

At the gate he looked out upon the road. It was a beautiful gleaming sheet of snow in both directions. Nothing had disturbed it for many hours. All was silent as death. Filth turned and looked up Veneering's drive.

That, too, was untouched; unmarked by birds, un-pocked by falling berries. Snow and snow. Falling and falling. Thick, wet, ice-cold. His bald head, ice-cold. Snow had gathered inside his collar, his cardigan, his slippers. Ice-cold. His hands were freezing as he grasped first at one yew branch and then another and, hand over hand, made his way up Veneering's drive.

'He'll have gone to the son,' said Old Filth. 'That, or there'll be some house party going on. Golfers. Smart solicitors.'

But the house was dark and seemed empty, as if it had been abandoned for years.

Old Filth rang the bell and stood in the porch and heard the bell tinkle far away, like Betty's at the rosewood dining-table in the Mid Levels.

And what the hell do I do next? he thought. He's probably gone to visit that fellow Christopher and they're carousing in the Peninsular. It'll be – what? Late night now. They'll have reached the brandy and cigars and all that vulgarity. Probably kill them. Hello?

A light had been switched on and a face looked out from a side window. Then the front door opened and a bent old man with a strand or two of still-blond hair peered round it.

'Filth? Come in.'

'Thank you.'

'No coat?'

'I just stepped across. I was looking out for a

taxi. For the White Hart. Christmas luncheon. Just hanging about. I thought I'd call and . . .'

'Merry Christmas. Good of you.'

They stood in the drear, un-hollied hall.

'I'll get you a towel. Better take off your cardigan – I'll get you another. Whisky?'

In the brown and freezing sitting-room a huge jigsaw puzzle only one-eighth completed was laid out across a table. Table and jigsaw were thick with dust. The venture had a hopeless look. 'Too much damn sky,' said Veneering as they stood looking down at it. 'I'll put another bar on. You must be cold. Maybe we'll hear your cab from here, but I doubt it. I'd guess it won't get through.'

'I wonder if I could use your phone? Mine seems to be defunct.'

'Mine, too, I'd guess, if yours is,' said Veneering. 'Try, by all means. I scarcely use it.'

The phone was dead.

They sat down before two small red wire-worms of the electric fire. Some sort of antique, thought Filth. Haven't seen one of those in sixty years. In a display case by the chimney-piece he saw a pair of old exotic earrings. The fire, the earrings, the whisky, the jigsaw, the silence and the eerily falling snow made him all at once want to weep.

'I was sorry to hear about Betty,' said Veneering.

'I was sorry about Elsie,' said Filth, remembering her name and her still and beautiful Chinese face. 'Is your son——?'

'Dead,' said Veneering. 'Killed. Army.'

'I am so very sorry. So dreadfully sorry. I hadn't heard.'

'We don't hear much these days, do we? Maybe we did too much hearing. Too many Hearings.'

Filth watched the arthritic, stooped figure shamble across the room to the decanter.

'Not good for the bones, this climate,' said Veneering.

'Did you never think of staying on?'

'Good God, no.'

'It suited you so well.' Then Filth said something very odd. 'Better than us, I always thought. Betty was very Scottish, you know.'

'Plenty of Scots in Hong Kong,' said Veneering.

'You two seemed absolutely welded there. Betty and her Chinese jewellery.'

'Oh, she tried,' said Filth, sadly.

'Another?'

'I should be getting home.'

It dawned on Old Filth that he would have to ask a favour of Veneering. He'd already lost a good point by coming round for help. Veneering was no fool. He'd spotted the dead-telephone business. It would be difficult to turn this round – make something of being the first to break the silence. Maturity. Magnanimity. Christmas. Hint of a larger spirit.

He wouldn't mention being locked out.

But how was he going to get home? The cleaning lady's key was three miles away and she wasn't coming in until the New Year. He could hardly stay here – good God, with Veneering!

'I've thought of coming to see you,' said Veneering. 'Several times, as a matter of fact, this past year. Getting on, both of us. Lot of water under the bridge and so on.'

Old Filth was silent. He himself had not thought of doing anything of the sort, and could not pretend. Never had known how to pretend. But he wished now . . .

'Couldn't think of a good excuse,' said Veneering. 'Bit afraid of the reception. Bloody hot-tempered type, I used to be. We weren't exactly similar.'

'I've nearly forgotten what type I was,' said Old Filth, again surprising himself. 'Not much of anything, I expect.'

'Bloody good advocate,' said Veneering.

'I'm told you made a damn good judge,' said Filth, remembering this was true.

'Only excuse I could think of was a feeble one. We've got a key of yours here, hanging in the pantry. Front-door key. Your address on the label. Must have been there for years. Some neighbours being neighbourly long ago, I expect. Maybe you have one of mine?'

'No,' said Filth. 'No. I've not seen one.'

'Could have let myself in, any time,' said Veneering. 'Murdered you in your bed.' There was a flash of the old black mischief. 'Must you go? I don't think there's going to be a taxi. It'll never make the hill. I'll get that key unless you want me to hold on to it for an emergency?'

'No,' said Filth. 'I'll take it and see if it works.'

*

On Veneering's porch, wearing Veneering's (frightful) overcoat, Filth paused. The snow was easing. He heard himself say, 'Boxing Day tomorrow. If you're on your own, I've a ham shank and some decent claret.'

'Pleasure,' said Veneering.

On his own doorstep Old Filth thought, Will it turn?

It did.

His house was beautifully warm but he made up the fire. He started thinking, of all things, about shark's-fin soup. There was a tin of it somewhere. And they could have prawns out of the freezer, and rice. Nothing easier. Tin of crab-meat, with the avocado, and parmesan on top. Spot of soy sauce.

Extraordinary Christmas.

Miss Mistletoe

Daisy Flagg was a parasite. Nothing wrong with that. Hers is a useful and ancient profession. In Classical times every decent citizen had a parasite. There were triclinia full of them. They flourished throughout Europe in the Middle Ages, though later demoted in England to the status of mere court jesters — demoted because your pure parasite does not have to sing for his supper. Not a bar. Not a note. His function is to sit there smiling below the salt cellar; not ostentatiously below it, but as *ami de maison*.

Now and then the parasite was noticed by those upstream above the salt, among the silver platters. Sometimes he was taunted and had to pretend to enjoy it. There was a Roman parasite who was teased by his host that he had only been invited because the host was having his way with the parasite's wife, and Ha! ha! ha! the parasite had to reply.

Professional parasites turn up even today in Italy

– at country weddings, sloping around at the back of the chairs, jollying people along at the wine-feast, nobody knowing who they are. The host sees they get their dinner.

Oh, the parasite was always a self-respecting fellow in his chosen profession. He knew he was easing the host's passage through this world and into the next. He was Lazarus raised up from the city gate. He was the rich man's ticket to heaven.

And there's something of him left still, especially at Christmastime, in England. We've all met him: the friend who's always at the Honeses', the Dishforths', the Hookaneyes'; who provides none of the spread, is no relation, doesn't do a hand's turn, seems to have little rapport with the rest of the company and is not particularly inspiring. Dear Arthur. Jim's friend Alan Something. Dorothy-she-was-something-to-do-with-your-grandmother. Mr Jackson (Beatrix Potter knew all about Mr Jackson). And it is excellent for all, because the host of any one of these people can say, 'And there'll be Mr Jackson of course as usual, God help us. But it *is* Christmas,' and Mr Jackson can say when the drunken invitation is at last extended at the office party on Christmas Eve, 'Oh, thanks, but at Christmas I always go to the Infills.'

And so it was with Daisy Flagg, the Christmas parasite known to the Infills behind her back as Miss Mistletoe. For years and years she had come to the Infills for Christmas, always arriving late following extensive devotions in her parish church some hundred miles away. She drew up in her ancient and decrepit car (which she maintained and serviced, patched and painted herself), its windscreen hazy, its tyres criminally worn, its back seat of rubbed-away, hollowed-out leather laden with awful presents. 'Sorry I'm late,' she would cry, springing through the back door into the kitchens, leaving the car in the middle of the frosty drive below the Renaissance urns on the terrace, all the eighteenth-century windows glittering in disdain. 'Happy Christmas, happy Christmas, all. *Terribly* sorry.' She would enter by the kitchens as a privileged member of the family, a family that now cooked its own Christmas dinner rather better, if more chaotically, than when there were cooks, and who because of the presence of Daisy Flagg/Miss Mistletoe behaved rather less badly among the bread sauce and the prune stuffing and the whirling machinery that resulted in the brandy butter than they otherwise would have done.

Daisy Flagg/Miss Mistletoe sat to table with her face in its permanent rictus grin, giving the impression of a delighted grasshopper in a paper hat. She was flat as a child, sideways almost invisible, transparent as a pressed flower. She was very clean. Her clothes seemed to have been boiled, her hair almost shampooed away. Her nails were scrubbed seashells. ('Some sort of guilt there,' said Laetitia the year she was doing Psychology.) Her shoes came from the jumble sales of her spiky church. They were often the old dancing slippers of dowagers, and once were gigantic Doc Martens found in a paper bag on the pavement in Victoria Street. Miss Mistletoe, who was very poor, had of course taken these straight to the police station. To the very top police station, Scotland Yard, just across the road. They had told her there that lost shoes were not their speciality and if they were her they'd keep them.

Miss Mistletoe wore miniskirts. Always. She must have acquired a great number of them some hot summer in the Beatles' time, for they were all very flimsy and her knees seemed to knock together beneath them in the icy wastes of Infill Hall. Her hair was always done for Christmas in a Cilla Black beehive *circa* 1975. It made her look steady and controlled; the permanent spinster, if the word still exists.

She ate voraciously, keeping the conversation flowing, trooping with the rest out of the dining-room to listen to the Queen. She ignored the children. She didn't like children. And she never walked the dogs in the park. Long ago she had been dissuaded from helping with the washing-up, for she tended to hop and giggle and drop the Infill Spode on the flagstones. 'Just sit and be comfortable,' they said, and disappeared with the retrievers into spinneys and woodlands and to trudge round the ornamental lake in the park.

Like a little bundle of sticks sat Miss Mistletoe beside the fire in the hall, across from vast old Archie, bibulous and asleep. She kept up her merry patter – the weather, her car, her journey, the Royal Family (not the scandals), *The Archers*, anything. When it was teatime she stayed on. Drinks time, she stayed on. Supper, she stayed on. A sort of pallet had always been laid out for her in a remote bedroom once occupied by a Victorian tubercular tweeny who was said to haunt it, though Miss Mistletoe never complained. Grey blankets and a towel were laid across this bed and these were always left so perfectly folded the next day that everyone wondered if Miss Mistletoe had slept in the bed at all. On Christmas night about midnight someone would say, the brandy flowing pretty free by now, though Miss Mistletoe never touched a drop of it, nor any alcohol ever: 'Come on, Daisy; you'd better stay the night.' 'Would that be all right?' was the awaited reply. 'It's *terribly* kind of you.' And she grinned and grinned.

The joke for Boxing Day was how to get rid of her. You couldn't say that everyone was going hunting because nobody did now. The horses were gone and the stables rented out as craft shops and mushroom beds. Laetitia still attended the meet in the village, but in her Lagonda because she was now a hunt saboteur. Nor could you say that everyone was going to the panto in Salisbury, because Miss Mistletoe's face seemed to say to them, 'Why didn't you get a ticket for me?'

Usually they eased her out about noon with the

second turkey leg and a wedge of the pudding and a tin of Boots' Lavender talcum powder which had always been her Christmas present. After waving her off they went back into the house and gathered up the presents she had given them and put them with the stuff for the NSPCC summer fair. They shrieked and groaned about Miss Mistletoe for the rest of the day.

Over the years some Infills died and some new ones were born but the numbers for the table at Christmas stayed more or less steady between fourteen and twenty. The year old Archie died, however, spread out peacefully beside the log fire one November morning early (though they didn't realise it till after *Newsnight*), the numbers had dropped. There would be only twelve, with Miss Mistletoe making the dreaded number of thirteen, and the oft-raised but never seriously considered question began to be asked outright: Do we have to have her?

'We could ask someone else and make it fourteen.'

'Who?'

Nobody could think.

'Well, we can't sit down thirteen. I'm not super-

stitious but, I mean, Christmas is a religious do.
That's when thirteen started.'

'It didn't,' said Laetitia, who was at present con-
cerned with Theology.

'We could say we were all going away.'

'She knows we never go away.'

'Well, we might. We could say we are all going
skiing.'

'Don't be silly. Letty and Hubert are over ninety.'

'We could say we're all going on a cruise.'

So they said they were all going on a cruise and
they sent Daisy Flagg a fat cheque (ten pounds)
and loving messages saying they knew that she
would have much more exciting places to go than
Infill Hall. Daisy Flagg wrote back on her lined
paper in her schoolgirl hand to say it was quite all
right, perfectly all right, and she'd be going to a
friend in Potter's Bar.

Sighs of relief.

'She's such a *bore*,' they said. 'How many years
have we had her? Twenty?'

'Oh no. Not twenty. It feels like twenty. Maybe
ten.'

'How old is Daisy Flagg?' someone asked as the

turkey was rather wearily dismembered, paper hats lying about the table and not on anybody's head. 'Forty? Fifty?'

'Could be any age. Could be only thirty-five. She was just a little girl in a first job when Mamma found her, wasn't she? Glove counter in the Army & Navy. Took a fancy to her. Isn't she still there?'

'No idea. I always thought she was something to do with Nannie.'

'Well, we needn't escape all afternoon anyway. Ghastly cold out there.' And they sat about indoors for hours, missing the Queen.

'We can hear her later,' said Jocelyn.

'If we must,' said Laetitia.

Somehow they didn't.

The evening hung heavy. Children fought over videos. Nobody would sit in Archie's splayed chair. The dogs lay around making smells because nobody would take them out. Nobody could face the second turkey leg. 'Next year,' said someone, 'better have the little creature back, don't you think?'

When, the following October, Laetitia decided to go and work for Mother Theresa in Calcutta (calling in at Rome on the way for a new handbag), the numbers came right again and the invitation was issued. Lady Infill surprised herself by saying, 'We missed you last year. You must tell us *all* you have been up to since.'

There was a little pause before the reply came, but it was an acceptance. Daisy Flagg said that she had missed them, too, and would be arriving as usual after attending the early celebration of Holy Communion. It was to be hoped, she added, as usual, that there would be no inclement weather for her hundred-mile drive.

And then, over the answerphone on Christmas morning – bleary-eyed Gervais pressing the button as he stood, yawning, over the kettle for the early-morning tea – came Daisy's voice saying she hoped it would be all right but she was bringing someone with her.

'Of course it's not all right,' screamed Lady Infill. 'Call her back immediately.'

'She's at church. The Early Celebration.'

'I don't care what celebration. She can't just land here with someone. We'll be thirteen again.'

'Maybe we could get in the vicar.'

'We don't know a vicar.'

'Maybe,' said Auntie Pansy hopefully, 'I could go to my London club?'

They quarrelled their way through breakfast, through the stuffing of the turkey, through the creation of gravies and bacon rolls, through the endless trimming and cleansing of sprouts. They sulked and fumed and drank a lot of wine and began to say that Daisy Flagg was a pain, always had been a pain, always would be, and why had they got her? They'd had the chance to be shot of her. They'd let it go. Who was she anyway? Nobody had ever known. It was all their mother's fault. Playing the eccentric *grande dame*. Years out of date. Egalitarian rubbish.

'Well we all know who your mother was,' said Sukey. 'Nobody.'

They sat at the table in disarray.

Turkey over, there was still no Daisy.

'Maybe she's had a crash on the motorway at last,' said someone.

But it was after half-past two by this time and

nobody quite dared to say, 'Let's hope,' for they were now disquieted.

'She'll swan in with the nuts,' said someone else. 'You'll see. She's probably bringing a man. She's probably married.'

But she wasn't married. Daisy Flagg the parasite never married.

Miss Mistletoe *married*? Ridiculous!

Towards the end of the orange and lemon sugar slices and the coffee, the limp wagging of the crackers, came the sound of the motor car upon the dying winter afternoon. It came into view, spluttering and clanking, between the stark branches of the avenue and jerked to a halt below the terrace.

And out of it sprang a shining-faced and stocky Daisy Flagg with a three-month-old baby in her arms, and she took her place at table and put this baby on her knee.

'So *terribly* late,' she said. 'Such *terrible* trouble with sparking plugs,' and she grinned. 'She's *terribly* hungry. D'you mind if I do this at table?'

And Miss Mistletoe upped with her smock and her T-shirt to reveal amazing bounty beneath.

Christmas Island

Soon after the last sticks of the rainforest had become firewood and the human community had perfected the technique of mechanical gestation and painless extermination and about four years after the discovery of the viruses that did away with the twentieth-century AIDS virus and the antibiotic-resistant diseases, the first woman gave birth to a child that bore little resemblance to anything that had been seen before.

It was a headless, armless pod of a creature, rubbery in texture yet of metallic appearance and the colour of unscoured pewter. In shape it was like a primitive pot or gourd and where on the human body you would expect neck and head there was a culinary rim.

Within the rim, about six inches down, the pot was sealed with a shallow, domed cranium, grey and pulsating like the head of a new-born child. Surrounding this palpitating soft fontanelle were coiled six or seven grey tubes the thickness of a sturdy macaroni.

These tubes, almost before the birth was complete, the cord being attached to the creature in much the usual way, began to move; to search and rise. They came wavering slowly upwards and proved to be between three and four feet long. Two had at their tip a gelatinous, limpid growth furnished with iris and pupil, and these came swaying like snakes and peering about them. Two more, tipped with grey, rubbery shells, swayed and tilted constantly towards every new sound. A further two were tough and eager hoses ending in a rubbery convolvulus-shaped flower like the cup at the end of a toy arrow. These cups sought out the human mother's nipple with an instinct so certain that the already terrified attendants at the birth vomited, screamed and fled.

A few brave souls tried somehow to detach these horrors, but without success. The suction cups fastened themselves like leeches to the supply of sustenance and like leeches dropped away only when sated. Curiously and most terribly of all, the mother of the new species (she was an aid worker on the island of La Réunion in the Indian Ocean, far from being a primitive society) displayed a powerful animal affection for her offspring and wept when it died, which it did after a few hours.

The communities into which the species now began to be born did their best to hide them, but soon they were appearing intercontinentally. They were not respecters of colour, class, creed or intellectual advancement. In centres of Science, specimens were secretly taken for laboratory analysis and in little-known tribes witch-doctors secreted parts, particularly the antennae, for use in spells. The parts, boiled or steamed and made into potions, changed hands for large sums of money but had little effect for good or ill. Human males in both kinds of society, if they were considered or considered themselves responsible for the conception of the creatures, tended to disappear. Mothers recovering from what in the early births was a particularly intense postnatal maternal passion now often ran mad when they had come to their senses. But, strangely, there was little suicide.

The monstrous progeny were buried in lonely places among the abandoned forest stumps, in deserts and quicksands, in shack-holes and old plague pits and in the cities of the dead; for it was soon discovered that they would neither melt nor burn.

About ten years after the birth of the first of these Spignoles (the name emerged from France) hesitant references to them began to appear, at first in the more dubious medical journals and in unreliable whispers on the Internet. The tone was apologetic, self-mocking. Risible and then less risible attitudes showed through in these reports and at last the subject reached the learned journals; but their content was still almost universally disbelieved.

The day came when the word Spignole appeared in the correspondence advertising symposia and medical conferences in out-of-the-way places (London, UK; Cambridge, UK and Mass.; MIT; Berkeley) and then on similar cards of invitation to weightier gatherings (Bangladesh; Galway, Ireland; Greenland). Simultaneously a new wave of the phenomena was rumoured.

Soon discussion became usual and internationally known. The creatures had started to take a more horrifying form; they were bigger, more slippery, of a more metallic appearance, colder to the touch. Hard and streamlined now, they were the colour of gun-metal and twice the size of a human baby. A type of medieval breastplate was sketched across the beetle body that was now equipped with genitalia and each creature possessed iron nipples, ample vaginal aperture and a huge metallic penis continuously erect. This Spignole did not die after only a few hours.

No mother now felt affection for her Spignole child, but horror. Throughout the world there surged a terror of parenthood. Sexual intercourse became loathsome, conception at first pitiable, then shameful and at length a crime. Lovers, the idea of physical contact in love, became obnoxious, chaste homosexuality almost holy and celibacy revered.

In order to preserve the human race and keep a force against the grey enemy now appearing in its hundreds and thousands in both hemispheres, hospitals demanded huge supplies of sperm. They sought it from men in wastelands and cities, from desert tribesmen and urban office workers, but soon the end results were all the same. Instead of the sweetly curled broad-bean-shaped natural human foetus inside the replica of the human womb, by the eighth month, soon in the sixth, and then at twelve weeks, headless pulp had developed into pure Spignole.

Shortly, women long past child-bearing as well as ten-year-old girls began to conceive, and without intercourse; and as the natural baby disappeared, so departed maternal love.

And then new, but always Spignole, life began to drop from women without warning, haphazard in the streets, in crowded churches, in bathrooms and bathing places – for Spignoles cannot drown – and in parliaments now in constant session throughout the world; in aeroplanes and spacecraft, in old untended gardens and along the beaches of the sea where women had gathered together for comfort. Age, caste, became meaningless. Peasants and royalty dropped Spignoles in ditch and palace. Pope Sheila VI dropped twin Spignoles in the Vatican. Wars ceased.

More was to come. As whole cities ran mad (strangely there were fewer suicides than might have been imagined) and the people threw themselves on God's invisible mercy, the Spignoles grew to a forbidding size and began to procreate alone. Their

68

dual mechanism was efficient and prolific. A two-year-old Spignole could spawn a dozen or twenty in an afternoon. Spignoles lay thick now in the gutters, crawling in the fields like a nightmare autumn. They covered the streets, gardens, beaches, hills: headless, flipperless seals. Rolling in heaps they began to swell, like vermicelli in soup.

Humans now made for the mountains, oceans, ice floes, deserts, but wherever they went the Spignoles were with them and before them.

Holy places were forgotten. The Jews deserted Jerusalem. Mecca fell silent. The Sea of Galilee, the Mount of Olives, the tomb of the Resurrection, were pasted with a thick coating of creatures who had never heard tell of a God and whom no living thing could conceivably bless.

A grey cast then fell across the blue planet. The stars watched as the lichen of the Spignoles ate up all the lands and the seas between. The occasional mountain top stood clear for a time. The Great Wall of China survived for a year. For a little longer than that the Himalayas rode sublime. But the army still advanced.

The survivors of the human race were pressed

upwards. Sometimes they were pressed to the rims of volcanoes, toppled over in their thousands, the Spignoles spilling after them to their own death. The people fell clutching their last treasures – photographs, jewels, sometimes a cross, a keepsake or a cheque-book. All went into the stew until the crater was filled.

It took seven more years for the earth to reach the point of death. Had there still been satellites to see it, they would have recorded a lightless, colourless tomb.

Except, at the last, for one pinprick spot. It lay in the middle of the Pacific Ocean, the Sea of Peace where in the twentieth century of earth its inhabitants, as the result of an insanity that had persisted until the Spignoles arrived, had experimented with methods to bring about their own destruction. This was known as Christmas Island, a name recording the birth of Christ; an atomic cinder on which many had died, others had prayed to die and others who had been able to come away had held death in their bodies to pass on to their children. This island was still just visible.

The Spignoles were all about it, however, coming

lazily forward on all sides, across the seas. Had their nature – a curious idea – been unknown, it might have been thought that they were weary now, or showing a salacious hesitation over the final gulp.

The atoll stood very small inside its Spignole frill; a scrap of earth, a dead palm tree, two last shabby vultures watching from a leathery leaf. At the foot of the tree was a huddle of eight or ten people, the last in the world.

The group was remarkable in that it included several generations who felt themselves bound together, a structure known as a 'family'. There was an old man, a middle-aged couple, a few young men and women, and, amazingly, a child. On the sand about them were some water containers and withered fruit. There was also a dog that looked as if it was dying, its head in the old man's lap. The limbs of these people were sharp as sticks under their rags, their eyes were huge with hunger and pain and covered in flies, but the old man was holding on to a book and one of the young men a musical instrument with broken strings. The little girl held a ball.

The ball was metal, and red, the sort used for the curious game of Boules, played in the little streets of country France on summer evenings and also, eastward of Christmas Island or westward, whichever way you choose to look, on the richly beautiful French island of Réunion.

The first arc of Spignoles was now welling forward over the beach towards the palm tree. Feelers fingered the sand. As far as the eye could see, though all eyes were now closed, antennae waved like mammal foam to every horizon. They tested, curled and tossed the air; they watched and listened for each human voice. The child's ball slipped from her fingers and rolled down the beach.

She opened her eyes to watch it roll. She saw it hit a rock. It bounced off the rock into the air and fell with a spreading clang on to the armoured back of a leading Spignole. The child sat up.

In the life of the child there had scarcely been music and this was not music now, but she clambered to her feet and trotted down the beach to the ball and dropped it again on the nearest creature's back; and again the sound rang out. The Spignole feelers were all about her feet, but she took the ball, she waded in amongst them, and dropped the ball again. And the sound was now like a gong.

So she moved forward, in among the Spignoles, and felt for the ball and slung it down again and laughed as the sound reverberated, echoed, shivered like a triumph, like a trumpet, like a conqueror. The humming glorious noise – the child was laughing too – shook the air like bells.

The Spignoles had halted. For ten thousand miles the antennae sank down limp. Nothing moved. The child threw the ball again and laughed again and began to walk towards the Spignoles, who appeared now to be at a little distance from her. She ran after them but they seemed to be fading down the beach. She cried, 'Oh, stop!'

But they were dying back fast, fast as cut flowers in a greenhouse. They were leaving a clean, unbroken ring around Christmas Island, like Fleming's saucer. In moments the beach, the beaches, were clear and lay silken and wet and the empty sea flashed blue for miles. The receding Spignole soup was a grey line, soon only a long uneven smudge on the horizon. And then even the horizon lay in simple blue and silver lines as the child had never seen it, and healthy great clouds came puffing up from beyond it. And, as they in turn dispersed, a serene moon came up out of the sea.

The child listened to the peaceful waves running up the beach towards her feet, moonlit waves like flounces of lace, stretching away and away along the shore. In a rock pool something moved. A fish, transparent, with a gold scarf for a tail, flourished its beauty in the water.

The people under the palm were stirring. The vultures had vanished. A small boat lay in the rocks. It looked old and brittle but sun-warmed and tight, with good oars. The group came weakly across the sand towards the boat. They helped each other in, and the boat floated away. The child, up in the prow on her mother's lap, listened to the music of the gentle night and watched the stars.

And earth was cleansed to its farthest shores, from the tips of the mountains to the depths of the sea.

Five Grotesques

Grace

Clockie Gosport had this great diamond in the back of his neck. Under the skin. At the top of the spine. In among all the wires that keep the show on the road. Just on the bone they break when they hang you. Clockie Gosport.

He was never a one to mention the diamond. Never. Very quiet and modest. A thoughtful man, born over Teesport in a street right on to the pavement, no back door or yard or running water or electric. And clean! Every part of it, including the old man, Old Gosport, Clockie's father, who was made to strip in the passage every night home from the Works and bath in the tin behind the screen.

She was a silent woman, Ma Gosport. She held the world together, packing in the lodgers head to tail in the upstairs double, the family all crammed about. She took in both day- and night-shift men, and every hour God gave she was washing and possing and mangling and hanging out bits of sheets.

She hung them out courtesy of Mrs Middleditch and the hook in her wall across the way. All was hygiene.

And this story went around. 'Clockie Gosport got a diamond in his neck.'

'Is it true you got a diamond in yer neck, Clockie?' (He was Clockie because way back someone had said: 'Like a watch. Watches has bits of diamond in them.')

Clockie always smiled. 'Now how could I have a diamond in me neck? They'd have me head off.'

That was as a grown man. At school he'd said nothing, just stared. He had these poppy eyes. The other kids said it was the diamond pushing them forwards. 'Gis yer diamond, Clockie. Come on, yer booger, gis yer diamond.' They would grab at him and Ma Gosport or the school teacher would wade in and cuff them all about.

Nobody cuffed Clockie, though. It was tradition. When Clockie had been five or six he'd been cuffed about at home for screaming and it was found to be the meningitis. There'd been silence all down Dunedin Street that night and folks coming and sitting quiet on the step and Old Gosport weeping. And Ma Gosport had been slapping and bashing the sheets in the back and then getting into her things for the walk to the Infirmary. Mrs Armitage and Mrs Middleditch had gone with her, the one excited, the other grim. They'd gone in order to support Ma Gosport back after the news, and Ma Gosport had stuck out her chin and never spoke once on the road, the three of them walking abreast in their hats and coats. She gave the women presents later. Mrs Middleditch she gave a jet brooch of her grand-mother's and Mrs Armitage she gave a steak pie.

For Clockie had recovered and, before Ma Gosport left the Infirmary, the doctor had called her in – 'No, just the mother, please' – and had put his arm round her.

'Mrs Gosport, your boy will get better and he's a lucky lad. We're very interested, though, in the foreign body lodged in the neck.'

'It's a diamond,' said Ma Gosport.

The doctor brooded. 'What exactly do you *mean* by a diamond, Mrs Gosport?'

'I don't know. It just happens sometimes in the family. There comes a bairn with the diamond. It means luck.'

'Have . . .' the doctor covered his face with his

hands and swirled them about, 'has anybody ever seen it?'

'No. Well, it's under the skin, isn't it?'

'We ought to examine it, you know. It is most fascinating.'

So she let them, but it was long ago before the war when X-rays were feeble, and what with air raids coming and hospitals so busy, Clockie's diamond went out of folks's minds.

Clockie was a poor scholar and slow talking. He never read. He grew very good-looking. Beautiful, really. He began work at the new chemical plant after the war, sweeping a road a mile long. He brushed with men to either side of him, a thin grey line, and every now and then a machine came along that gobbled up the dirt. Then the men stopped, drew on a fag, slung it away, lined up again, swept on. At the end of the mile they knocked off for a can of tea and walked back and started again. It didn't worry Clockie. It was regular work and you could listen. It was surprising what you heard.

''Ere, Clockie,' they said on wet days, 'how 'bout releasing this diamond and we all get off to Paris?'

They'd glance at the back of his neck now and then, but it was always covered by the sweat-rag his mother gave him, boiled clean, each morning. They'd not have thought of touching it.

When he got a girl, though, she wanted to touch it, of course she did. She was Betty Liverton, dumpy little thing, all charm.

'Welsh,' said his mother. 'Not to be trusted.' Betty had her hands round his neck second time out.

Clockie wasn't sweeping any more. He'd graduated first to the suction machine and found affinity with all forms of mechanical life. Now he was the feller with the screwdriver round the ethylene plant and everybody shouting for him.

He'd moved up to the mechanics' canteen, where Betty Liverton washed the mugs. Short little legs, lovely chest, freckles, soft eyes – she watched him with his curly hair. Big feller, Clockie.

Then down Ormesby Lane, by the bit of wood and stream that's not overlooked, they lay down beside the kingcups and put their hands on each other and she screamed.

'What is't?' He was undoing her dress.

'Stop it. Dear Lord, it's true!'

'What's true?' His blue pop-eyes were shining. He wasn't laying off for long.

'It's true. In the back of yer neck. The diamond.'

He pushed her down. (And him thought slow!)

'Get off. I want to see. It's right on the surface. I could bite it out.'

'Does it bother you, then?' He took both her wrists in one hand and held them in the grass above her head. She was amazed.

'It doesn't bother me. I just never could believe it.'

She forgot the diamond. All she could think of that night in her bed as she played back her deflowering beside Ormesby Beck was that it couldn't have been his first time.

'Was it yer first time?' she asked when they were married.

'It come natural,' said Clockie.

She became the envy of the street with her sleepy honeymoon looks.

They got a couple of rooms up the road and Ma Gosport made the best of it, taking in another lodger and then another when Old Gosport went at last, spotless, to his coffin. She never liked Betty Liverton.

Clockie stayed tranquil, so tranquil that it was a puzzle to some that after the first days of marriage were over and Betty grown brisk there were so quickly two girls and a boy, all the image of their father. It was only image, though. There was not his temperament, not the peace of him. They grew up to be rubbish.

'Well, their mother's rubbish, isn't she?' said Ma Gosport. 'She got tired of him. There wasn't a thought between them.'

Clockie grew quieter still after the kids were flown and Betty went off with Alan Middleditch. 'That's Wales for you,' said Ma Gosport just before she died.

And Betty drank port-and-lemons down the golf club and was always well away by eight o'clock, talking of her husband who thought he had a diamond in his neck.

Clockie used to walk the beaches of the estuary in time, among the sharp sand-grasses and the grey flowers. He met folks there. Once he met a daft fairground girl, white-headed. He was an old man now and they lay quiet in the sand dunes. The girl lay beside him like a pearly fish.

She said: 'You've got this thing in the back of your neck. It'll be a diamond.'

'Have you heard tell of this, then?'

'Oh, aye,' she said, 'long since. There's them with the diamond.'

'Where you from, girl? Which country?'

But she didn't seem to know.

He fettled for himself at home till his hip went and he had it done and a date fixed for the other one, but by then he was failing. He was no great age, but old for a man of his history always living in the reek of the Works. The road he'd swept was a bit of a motorway now, the chimneys all plumed with gases. In hospital he grew poorly and they sent for his children and a son came he'd not seen for years bringing a little one with him called Meg, golden-haired. Before they left, Clockie put out a calloused old hand and touched her hair. He put his hand under the hair and at the back of the neck he felt the diamond. They looked at one another.

The doctors had wanted him to have the foreign body removed on the occasion of the first operation and they were still on about it now. 'It can't be doing you any good, Grandad. Is it First War shrapnel? You're a lucky old devil.'

'I wasn't born First War,' said Clockie. 'It's said to be a diamond.'

Well, they were full of it. Clockie lay thinking of Meg.

''Ere,' he said late one night, 'Nurse. Tell them OK. I'll have it done. They can take out the diamond when I'm under the knife for the hip. They tell me it's but a matter of lifting it off. Now then, if it does turn out to be a diamond, it's to be for Meg. She'll not need it, she's got her own. But you're to tell her I said.'

The surgeons laughed their heads off. One said he'd once had a patient with a tin of Harpic stuck up his bum. They put off the hip for a week, until the big man could come down from Newcastle.

'Let's have another look at the little lass,' said Clockie, and when she was brought he sent her father out and said: 'Meg, you and I are old friends. What's this behind the curtains?'

And she said: 'It's a diamond.'

'That's right,' said Clockie. 'You'll be grand. You'll always be grand, girl. You and me, Meg, we know the ropes of living and dying. We're safe, girl.'

The next day they did the hip successfully and nipped out the diamond from the back of the neck and they killed him of course.

The thing rattled into the kidney-dish, a vast great lump of glass. They all went mad. One doctor who was South African said he'd seen many an uncut diamond but never one as fine as this. The great man said: 'You know, this could be a diamond.'

Then Clockie began to die and it was all hands to the pump, and in the midst of the red alerts going off, and Clockie going out, a soft young nurse (she was an Armitage) cleared away the kidney-dish and washed the diamond down the sluice. It was a wide-lipped sluice without a grille and so the diamond was taken straight down into the Middlesbrough sewers and then far away out into the North Sea, where it is likely to be washing around for ever.

When she was told of her grandfather's death, Meg put her face in the back of his chair to savour the nice salt smell of him. She put her thumb in her mouth, and the other hand she wound round to the back of her neck to make sure of the diamond.

Light

In the furthest Himalayas there was a child born with a single eye. You might think that this would have been to its advantage, for a single eye is frequently considered a sign of the greatest holiness. But this was the rumoured kingdom of Imlac and its religion was not altogether orthodox. It was a country even further and higher than Ladak, across wastes of unmarked snows, up a precipice with a float of clouds halfway up it and at the top of a vast tableland, scarcely peopled, scarcely visited, because of the avalanches sent by its gods, in particular the Snow Leopard.

The Snow Leopard was said to send the avalanches to kill interference from the outside world, from politics, accepted religions, medicine and foreign artistic endeavour (they were a conceited people), and, some said, as punishment for their sins.

But the holy idea of the single eye shining from

the forehead had filtered into Imlac in a related interpretation and what made the plight of the baby, a little girl called Keril (which means shadow), hazardous and unfortunate was that her mother had promised her to the priests to be their goddess.

In the region of Imlac, as in Nepal today, a little girl, the most beautiful that could be found, was taken at two years old into a closed monastery and worshipped there as a goddess until she was about thirteen, or until the day of her first menstruation. When this occurred she was sent home. Women came to undo the tight bun of her hair and led her back to her family again, a family completely strange to her. She came back illiterate. For ten years she had been taught nothing except how to sit utterly still as, hour by hour, day by day, year by year, the monks filed past her, bowing and chanting and worshipping. At other times honoured supplicants from the world outside approached and reverently spread at her feet presents, which the monks then removed.

In Imlac there were secret initiation ceremonies for these little girls, as there are today in Katmandu, and it is said that potions given to encourage the goddess's docility were powerful and carefully guarded. Certainly when she was taken through the city on her throne, hung between poles and carried by a full football team of chanting, ruby-red, orange-helmeted monks, she stared blankly ahead as if there were other and sad scenes before her kohl-encircled eyes. A third great eye painted on the forehead glared out black, vermilion and gold beneath her jewelled triple crown. Bumping about unsmiling above the heads of the crowd, the child looked like a small bronze statue, quite unable to recognise her mother and family who would be somewhere there watching, filled with pride but often weeping.

In Imlac it was beginning to be harder to acquire one of these goddesses – as it is in Katmandu today. Mothers were refusing and the priests were troubled. The given reason for refusal was always unworthiness for such an honour, but the real reason was that when the goddess was returned home she was a useless zombie, unable even to clean a floor, make a cheese, bake a loaf and accustomed to continuous admiration.

And marriage was uncertain. Cobwebs of magic still hung about these girls. They were said to have secret knowledge and husbands tended to die mysteriously in the first matrimonial year (which is still said to be true in Nepal) and snakes were said to issue from the girls' vaginas during intercourse.

The mother of Keril had for some years been living in the remotest part of the kingdom to try to escape the notice of the monks, for twice now she had had the misfortune to produce daughters of exceptional beauty, twice the monks had sent for them and twice she had refused. These daughters had died.

She lived a hard life now out in the furthest and coldest part of the region, where it was said there was only one day a year of summer, eight months of weather so hard that no other tribe could endure them and four months when the cold drove even this community underground to live in deep chambers cut into the rock, clamped down under iron lids. The one day of summer, however, was of delirious beauty.

It was out of exhaustion that the woman promised the monks her next daughter, and they told her it would be her passport to heaven. There, they said, she would find summer every day in the territory of the Snow Leopard whose realm is of no known world.

So the baby was conceived as she knew it would be. There is little help for it in an underground village with nothing else to do for four long months and everyone in a heap and who knows who it is who fumbles for you in the dark. The mother prayed constantly that the child would be a boy, that if it were a girl it might be ugly and that the Snow Leopard would bless her whatever happened.

The first two requests were not granted. The child was female and very beautiful. It took time to determine that her blindness constituted the answer to the third request, the blessing.

For blind she seemed. The eyes were obviously there, but closed. The long, tilted, lashless Himalayan eyelids were so delicately drawn that they looked as if they might be prised apart by the gentle stroking of a fingertip. But no. This was illusion. The lines were unbreakable, the pale and luminous skin integral to cheek and brow, the gentle mounds of the hidden eyeballs as smooth and seamless and sealed as small well-poached eggs.

It was several days before the mother found the

third and operative eye that lived down in the baby's throat, an eye that presumably the child must close whilst feeding, an eye that flashed at the mother one morning as she looked down at the sweetly sleeping bundle strapped warmly to her breast as they stood on the windy plateau. The eye flashed as the cold sun shone on to the triangular mouth, which was opening in a yawn.

The mother died quite soon afterwards, not necessarily altogether from shock, for she was already worn out, but the revelation was certainly not conducive to survival.

The grandmother took the child then, and when the emissary of the monastery appeared two days later to take the baby she gave no hint about the hidden eye. She had kept it secret from everyone. And yet a whiff of something unsavoury had somehow reached the city – something sinister about the new goddess on the plateau who seemed always to be asleep.

When the emissary looked down at the child's sealed eyes, he took his leave at once without her, not even pausing to make the ritual tests of purity, the cleansing of the orifices: the flour for the ears, the lamp for the eyes, the incense for the nose, the herbal ointments for the sexual organs and, most importantly, the washing of the mouth with rice. He swirled off and fled, the eyeless infant lying golden and almost divinely fair on the smelly black goat-skins near the mouth of the winter dwelling.

The baby, of course, knew nothing of her beginnings. She never knew that she had been carried in the funeral procession of her mother, or that it had been then suggested that it would be better for a blind girl to be put out beside her to die on the mountain and be picked clean by the birds.

As she grew older she did not greatly miss her two eyes, for (sworn to secrecy by her grandmother) she held her mouth open whenever she felt like it, sometimes in wonder, sometimes out of curiosity, sometimes for convenience when she was sewing or for safety when she was on the icy slopes. All this seemed normal, if very slightly retarded.

And can you believe that in such a society nobody knew about the eye in the throat except the grandmother? Well, it is true. Keril was a silent child and the grandmother was not a gregarious woman and kept her apart. She was slightly feared, too, the old creature, humped-down, hook-beaked, dressed always in rusty black and brown instead of the brilliant costume of the land. She was given to talking and muttering to herself sitting out on the hillside, the only one who did not seem to long for the one summer's day. In all possible weathers she would sit gazing down for hours at the two great converging rivers that could be seen, sometimes even heard, thundering between drifts in the clouds. Even Keril, who showed little emotion about anything, was afraid of her grandmother.

She grew up, then, almost as remote from her tribe as if she had been the little goddess. She was different. For a start she was clean. Her nose did not run with thick, green mucus that left a pale track down a filthy cheek and was never wiped away. Nor did she wheeze and cough and die before she was ten, as one in six of the other children did. Her voice was soft and she moved quietly about on pretty feet. She wound up her hair with delicacy as she grew up and arranged it high in her fan-shaped headdress of gold coins that were to be her dowry, in an almost royal way. She sang to herself, as she sat with the goats beside her grandmother, in a voice that made the hardest men fall silent. She seemed untroubled by her hidden abnormality. Watching her gaze open-mouthed at the sky above, down at the great valley or up and away above her home to the tablelands towards Tibet where the yetis live, they said, 'It's as if she sees.'

'It's as if she sees,' they said uneasily to the grandmother.

'She is praying to the Snow Leopard,' said she.

As a baby Keril had never cried, at least not visibly, and as a girl she grew to be brave and self-sufficient. Nobody ever saw down her throat. She ate with small bites, never had tonsillitis, was fortunate enough in having no toothache, and if she had a little bit of goat's sinew stuck between her teeth she flew at once, and only, to her grandmother. She made sure never to laugh loudly, sing in company or let her jaw drop in surprise. After babyhood she never again yawned without politely covering her mouth and she sat away from the village, listening to the wind and the rivers, opening her mouth only to the turning eagles above her, allowing herself to laugh and gape only at the yetis when they came blundering up close. Yetis often slink about these far villages and are given pet names. They have to be shooed away from eating the sunflowers that sprout into glory on the one summer's day.

Keril's danger began with puberty and the following months of darkness in the underground tomb. By long tradition boys and girls were separated down there at night until it was thought that the girls were old enough for marriage or childbearing. Keril, at fourteen, was still too young and had managed to keep a private space for herself between the sour-smelling, skin-hung wall and the bony back of her grandmother. But in the soft light of the butter-lamps and the heat and reek of the place, particularly of the butter with which everyone was daubed like oven-ready chickens (Keril did not lard herself like the rest, yet she never felt cold and her skin remained soft and the colour of ripe corn), there were men to whom this beautiful girl was becoming an obsession. They showed it by shouting at her, flinging hard work at her, pressing her hands down on hot pots, saying she did not earn her keep and made the excuse of her blindness. She brought them bad luck, they said. Why had they kept her? Why did they keep her? In the night she would awaken to furious quarrels between them and her grandmother, who kept them off with threats of demons and the wrath of the Snow Leopard.

There was a village boy who could have any girl he wanted. There always is. He was eighteen years old with beautiful narrow black eyes and he was fascinated by Keril's blindness because he felt that even sitting in her darkness she could see him; that she knew him. He was angry because she hid from him more than from the others. And he was angry because he knew that she wanted him.

When the open weather came he watched her on the plateau. When the glorious summer day drew near and it was the annual festival of the goddess down the mountain, he asked the grandmother's permission to take the girl with him.

And when this was refused he took some coins and goatskins, dressed himself in the wonderful clothes of his region – the diamond-patterned woollen stockings, the midnight-blue wool shirt, the tunic of scarlet and purple with the white wool skirt beneath, the white cuffs turned back like a Puritan's (but buttoned with knobs of jade) – and made off alone. After three days he returned with a necklace for Keril made of sky-blue turquoises and the village girls hated her because she could not even see it. She sat there fingering it, holding it high, open-mouthed, until the grandmother came and took it away.

And then the summer's day arrived. The underground chambers were cleared and the goats led out from them, and the butter-lamps and the dung and the skins and the gallons of pale, weak whisky restored above ground, and all the stew and darkness of winter blew away. Flowers, like miracles, appeared in the melting snow.

The boy looked endlessly at Keril as she sat, still mittened and booted and shawled but lifting her face to the sun and smiling. While the grandmother was rearranging their quarters for the period above the ground, the boy came and took Keril by the wrist, away behind the rocks, pulled her down and kissed her. She did not struggle even when his mouth took the light away from her and his tongue came into her mouth urging and probing about like a live animal. And it came upon the eye.

She had of course closed the eye, but he felt it.

He rolled off her, took her face between his two dark, goat-boy's hands and pressed until her mouth was forced open. He hauled her small head towards him and shook it, and down in the throat the eye opened, liquid and gleaming.

He screamed. He screamed and fled, leaving her lying. Much later the grandmother came with water and alcohol and made her drink it.

The grandmother knew that the eye within was weeping, for the girl choked and gulped and clung to her. The grandmother knew too that Keril would have to die. Nothing so terrible, secret and watchful as Keril's eye had ever been known.

So the next day, with the village all standing close together, far away and silent, and the boy nowhere to be seen, the grandmother and Keril set off upwards into the highest places where it is always winter and there is no life that can survive except for the few animals who live a paralysed existence as sustenance for the Snow Leopard. If, of course, the Snow Leopard exists, for few claim to have seen him.

The two women, one black and bent, one upright and slender as a summer fern, set off up the mountain plateau and over the table-top snows. They passed a couple of yetis on the way who ambled up on their great feet, but Keril did not notice them and the grandmother eased them away with the palm of her hand as if they were nuzzling cattle. On the two women went, until the going became too hard for the old woman and they stopped and looked back. A whirling, untimely storm seemed to be gathering below. 'Go back now,' said the girl. 'I shall go on until there is somewhere to rest. Then I shall cover my face and go into the dark.'

So the old woman went hobbling down the mountain and night fell. The girl sat in the cleft of the rocks in her ceremonial clothes but without the blue necklace. Her hair was coiled round the fan of her headdress, which did not now jingle and jump with the gold-coin dowry left her by her mother. This too had been taken from her. For hundreds of miles about her the mountains turned violet and orange-red, lemon and sickening green, as the night fell, and she wrapped herself in her woollen shawl and waited to die.

But as the dawn came she was still not dead. All night she had sat, tranced as a child goddess in the thin, almost non-existent air. In the cold that should have burned her body into the rock, she had sat neatly, quite warm, breathing easily, and as the sun rose she dropped the shawl from her face and turned her eyelessness up to it. She heard a soft sound near her and the Snow Leopard on his silken feet approached and brushed her shoulder and snuffed her cheek. Then he licked the sealed eyelids and her eyes flew open to the sun.

At the fullness of light she screamed, and as she screamed the third eye shot out of her mouth and lay in the snow, a wet, black beetle. It rolled away from her and gathered snow and within a moment it had gathered enough to be the size of a man's head, and then a yeti's head and then the dome of a huge round Dzong. And then it was the size of a rotunda temple on the plain, and then it was the size of the great monastery of the city.

Then the snow of the whole mountainside seemed to be sucked towards it and, high as a range of hills, it rolled over the precipice, gathering snows a mile wide and hundreds of metres deep, and down it dropped, surging like oceans, to engulf the village.

Then it roared on to engulf the realm below, the

city itself, the temples, the markets, the streets of noble, painted houses. Then it took mile upon mile of little farms, with their gardens of herbs and roofs shiny with capsicums like splashes of blood. It rolled even further down the valleys of serpentine rice terraces, to where the dark-green corn grew among apple trees that blossomed and fruited twice a year among the meadow flowers. And it covered them too.

Only the rivers it could not subdue, and so it merged with them and soon the great valley kingdom was water, green, icy water, deep as the sea.

The girl Keril survives, however. Occasionally an intrepid and partly snow-blinded explorer catches sight of her riding the sky on the Snow Leopard's back, her eyes as clear and beautiful as the stars.

The Girl with the Golden Ears

Eglantine Fosche-Grille (Egg), editor of *Psi*, the dreamboat fashion publication of the western world, had discovered there was golden hair growing out of her ears.

It had started by sprouting in tufts and then in little beards. Then it began to show its desire if left to itself to go cascading down each side of her neck in rippling waterfalls. Goodness knows how long it would have grown or where it would have got to if Eglantine had not kept it under control with secret scissors and a will of hardest steel.

She was American and famous. She was not so much tough in her profession as metallic. She was six foot two, flat all over, with a long, pale face that had become as identifiable in the press as Picasso's sad clown. She had a small head on a long neck, more ostrich than Egg. She wore black. Always. Her eyes were the only part of her that did not lie flush. Well, there was the long, long nose but it was

Picassoesque and low-slung, too. Her eyes were large, round ostrich eyes, also black. The hair of her head she had always kept cropped straight and black, and shiny like a tiny leather cap or the poll of an oyster-catcher.

Her legs were magnificent and since she had for years ruled over *Psi* in total dominion there is no need to describe the impeccable excellence of her clothes. Eglantine Fosche-Grille, Ancient Egyptian in her confident geometry, wore her clothes as upon a frieze in the Valley of the Kings. Her inconspicuous correctness made everybody else, however austere or scruffy-looking or silky, depending on the vagaries of the times, look like Christmas-tree fairies. All the great couturiers claimed her with nods and winks as their own.

The clothes were in fact all home-made by the woman Egg lived with and had lived with for twenty years since their student days at the London College of Art. A fat little inarticulate English soul from West Yorkshire who toddled about their apartment in old shoes, Puppy Warwick was as broad as she was long, short-legged, pig-eyed and possessed of an unfortunate chest and high stomach. Puppy cooked for Egg, too, when Egg was at home. She made good English puddings and thick gravies and custard, which Egg consumed in pints, never adding to her negligible weight by so much as an ounce.

Nobody of Egg's knew about Puppy Warwick. Egg had had several statutory love affairs with men and some said there had once been a marriage, though lightly worn and soon discarded. Some did say that they believed there was a woman about somewhere, but nobody really knew.

There was not one thing that Puppy did not know about Egg, except the ear hair – and this she did not guess. Egg had always spent hours in the bathroom and now, at forty-five, it was not surprising that she had begun to spend longer. For quite six months now not a scrap of snipped-off hair had been spotted by Puppy. Egg had perfected the wrapping of it in tiny parcels and the dropping of them in the trash cans on the subway. Her new habit of travelling to work by public transport and not by cab – she, rich as the President – was considered a notable eccentricity and she soon became a feature of the subway, sometimes photographed there for the society magazines. She stood – never sat – in her black clothes, black and gold jewellery and (since the ear hair) a series of wonderful turbans that had quickly become the rage and greatly improved the economies of India and Morocco.

Lately Puppy Warwick had died. This meant that Egg had more freedom in the bathroom to deal with the hair and could pop it, wrapped, in the bin under the kitchen sink. She had had a go or two at getting rid of it down the drains, but this had not been successful. Once it had clogged up the waste-disposal and she had had to spend an hour with forks and couture hat-pins to save it from the eyes of the Jamaican maid. It was very nice hair, the ear hair. Lustrous stuff. It seemed to have a private life of its own. How strange, Egg thought, that it is usually baldness that a woman most fears.

She repeated such apparently subjective thoughts to herself without any expression crossing her face. At work she was, as ever, always apparently undistracted, moving with Olympian demeanour. She lunched and dined, attended the theatre, travelled abroad, took her vitamin juices, ordered more and more turbans. She left her hairdresser and, at first nervously, began to cut her scalp hair herself and found she was good at it. Even when turbaned, she never allowed any close-up photographs. Strangely, after the ritual daily clippings the insides of her ears never showed any sign of stubble.

Nobody ever touched Egg's ears. In fact, nobody ever touched Egg anywhere. She had had no lovers for years, much relieved that she had achieved enough well-documented affairs to satisfy herself and others that there was nothing the matter with her and that she could use her body fully if she so wished. She had never much enjoyed the physical demands of these liaisons anyway, had lain still and ice-bound, legs apart like a gym-lesson, staring and thinking determinedly of costings, pull-outs and mergers. Her men had always left her knowing nothing about her and not at all disturbed by the fact, for they were pleased at having got so far with someone so obviously discriminating and mysterious. They sent flowers the next morning. They were all so much the same that at parties and conferences she couldn't remember which ones she had done it with and which she hadn't. As for Puppy, her daring (at that time) undergraduate passion for Puppy had soon been over.

Puppy's death had been sudden: cancer diagnosed and victorious inside three weeks. She and Puppy – Puppy only at Egg's insistence and long ago – had belonged to an association that believes in the elimination of ritual from death and guarantees removal of a body from your home address within the hour. No anguish of funeral. No unhealthy tears and laughter of a wake. A ring at the bell. Faceless men. Down the fire escape. A notice in the paper. That was that. Egg had no religious beliefs or sense of the spirit and Puppy had no relations. A prayer-book, well-thumbed, found by Egg when she threw all Puppy's things away, surprised her.

And Puppy, it turned out, had other secrets as startling as Egg's bathroom scissors. Egg found herself answering the telephone of an evening to sobbing and sometimes angry people of both sexes and once the door of the apartment to a very young man, distraught and beautiful in huge Doc Martens, a baseball cap and tears. Puppy's will had brought by then its own surprises, for she had left Egg nothing, not even a note. Egg received a letter from the boy the day after his visit apologising for hysteria, asking if she could spare a photograph of

Puppy when young and suggesting a lunch so that they could celebrate his wonderful inheritance. Egg remained calm, refused the invitation, refused to speculate on how Puppy had made her fortune, disregarded the request for the photograph and bought a cat.

She bought a cat in her own image, a cat like her, so that the world was amused. Somebody did a portrait of them together and there was a party for its unveiling. Sycophants drooled. It was a black thing, the cat, sinuous and intelligent, with remarkable eyes. Its ears were patrician, almost transparent, and it sat on Egg's windowsill in her black-and-cream office with the sun streaming through them, sometimes industriously licking its paws and taking a swipe round the back of the ears so that they shone like wax. Egg began to notice that the sun revealed a hazy fuzz like morning mist inside the cat's ears. She had bought the cat on a sunless day.

The cat went everywhere with Egg, and on the subway it crouched in a bag of richest crocodile, the zip not quite done up to leave a purpose-made aperture for the head. Perfectly safe. The head looked interestedly around and got itself into all the glossies. The population of New York was enchanted. *Psi* said, 'It's the dead spit of you, Egg. All it needs is the turban. What's its name?' She called it only Cat or Pusscat and then nothing at all. Soon she tried not to see it, for she had begun to notice that the morning mist in its ears was becoming now quite dense fog. And as the cat's ear hair grew thicker, so it seemed to her did her own.

Her own ear hair was now very luxuriant indeed. She had become expert at cutting it, shaving it off, smoothing out the interiors of her impeccable shells, rinsing them with lotions, drying them with sterile muslin gauze. She had made a collection of beautiful little razors and scissors – but suddenly, one morning about a month after Puppy's body, unhouselled, unaneled, had been hauled off to its anonymous bonfire, she woke in horror.

She had got rid of the huge double bed in which for many years, before the ear hair, she and Puppy had slept across a Gobi of linen. She had bought for herself a narrow single couch inlaid with malachite and lapis and hung about with plum silk frills, swags and curtains like a Moroccan bordello. In this she now awoke one day to find that the hair in the night had gone totally out of control. Long, slippery ropes of it flowed from each ear, fanning out over the pillows and rippling like living creatures all over the quilt.

And the cat was in the midst of it, playing with it and smiling. It was pouncing upon it, tangling the hair with its claws, gnawing and tearing at it malevolently with its teeth.

That was the cat's last morning. An hour or so later it had wriggled out of the carelessly fastened bag and been turned to juice under a truck outside the *Psi* building.

'Egg's lost her cat,' they shouted around. 'Splatto. She's devastated.'

'Egg devastated? Do me a favour! She went right into a meeting. She's there now.'

'Can that woman never suffer?'

'Egg? Not even in her sweetest dreams.'

'What – Egg? Dreams?'

But Eglantine Fosche-Grille was having dreams. She was dreaming of Puppy, Puppy smiling and nodding at her in the night. Puppy holding out a pan of

Yorkshire pud in one hand and a great, ugly English handbag in the other, stuffed with money all spilling out. 'What can I get you, Egg?' she was saying, watchful, sneering, resentful, snide. 'Would you like me to shampoo all your beautiful hair?'

After one such dream of terrible clarity Egg woke with the hair crawling about all over her face, and she vomited. She had only just bundled the hair into a quite sizeable paper parcel when the Jamaican maid arrived and found her shivering in a blanket. No, she was not going in to work.

'Save us and help us, Lord God in heaven,' said the maid. 'I'll get you rum and milk and I'll take up this rubbish,' and she picked up the loose parcel and nearly dropped dead when her ice-cold, cryptic employer screamed, 'Put that down. *Now*! Thank *you*!'

Egg knew that she must have help. But what? A doctor? She was not sick. A psychiatrist? Her mind was entire. This was a totally physical manifestation. A trichologist?

She would find one, write anonymously, give a box number, enclose many dollars. She scanned the pages of *Psi* itself and found that several of the best-qualified trichologists lived in her own palatial block. She made an appointment with one of them, padded to his brass plate, stood in his silent corridor; at length, padded away.

For she would have been recognised. Her extraordinary face was known in Paris, New York, London. She must find a rural trichologist somewhere in the wild.

Egg took leave and went to Maine and sat out on rocks and ate lobsters and watched seaweed floating in the pools, like hair. There didn't seem to be many trichologists in Maine, but a couple of people from the publishing world walked hand in hand beside the ocean with a sidelong glance at her, thrilled when she gave them a small smile. They said, 'Love the swimming cap, Egg. The inset headphones.'

For the hair was growing now so fast that it had to be arranged in coils, imprisoned in plastic bun bags, growing by daylight as well as in bed. All day long she felt it thickening up, moving beneath the headgear. By lunchtime she was having to retire in order to braid it. She tried dyeing her own black hair to the ear hair's colour in the bathroom basin.

It wouldn't. Then she tried dyeing the ear hair black. But it wouldn't. She could neither copy nor eliminate the harvest corn.

'Don't they make you deaf, those ear-muff things?'

'Yes,' she said, 'a little. It's a new thing, though. It'll be big.'

She sat there on the edge of the ocean arranging scenarios in her head, fashion premières where she launched – imposed – the wonder of female ear hair on a waiting world. Why not? After all, how ridiculous is hair in history: the great fat rolls and sausages of the eighteenth century flopping in rows down the back and sides; women in cones of grey wig hair set up on scaffolding, stuffed with paste, now and then tenanted by lice and even mice, for goodness' sake. Wigs that needed rooms to themselves to be powdered. *The History of Hair*, she thought, *The Mystery and Lunacy of Hair Fashion and the Human Form*. Old hat, she thought, then: Punning, so help me! I'm nuts. I'm finished. Over the hill.

She went to California and enquired for a tricho-logical consultation in Los Angeles, where normality slumbers. She took courage and samples and notes of different rates of growth and lustre. The trichologist was bald, with eyes that he thought hypnotic. 'But you are *bald*,' she said, and he said, 'Sure; it's to show you you don't have to worry about one thing in this world. All things can be got past. I once knew an orchestral conductor with no arms.'

'This is a case of too much, not too little.'

'No problem. Let's get you on the computer. Hey – aren't you Egg Schwartzkopf-Cuttle – Something? Egg? *Psi*?'

So Egg went away to Italy in the sunshine and looked at easy careless girls with beards under their arms, and to India, where there were shameless moustaches. But all of them had empty ears. She went to South America, where she'd heard there were some Peruvian women who could knit their pubic hair into garments. She found them and squatted beside them and they looked at her from beneath their bowler hats and said, 'Hey – aren't you the fashion editor of *Psi*?'

On the tiny plane from Acapulco, travelling she had

forgotten to enquire where, not sure from where she had started out – she must look at her ticket; oh God, she was tired – she sat gaunt and withdrawn. She refused refreshment, conversation, closed her eyes when they spoke of safety regulations, managed to unfasten her seat-belt when they were suddenly scooped up by a great hand and tossed about the sky above Brazil. Lightning played about the wheels that hung below the antique undercarriage, but the plane danced on. No such luck.

She was wearing a roomy turban topped with gauze scarves under a vast Raj hat. The concept had not been treated with much enthusiasm at *Psi*. There had even been sniggers. *Psi* had been going down lately. Egg's second-in-command was aggressively at work in her absence. There were rumblings of Egg's decline.

But she cared nothing for it. Nothing now engaged her except the relentless onslaught of the hair. 'What other work could I do? What other life could I live?' she asked someone or something. Was she asking Puppy?

For years she had informed Puppy, not enquired. As Puppy had slopped about life, doing nothing, she had begun to detest her – her watchfulness, her reticence, her ugliness and – now she knew – her deviousness and straight nastiness. A parasite. All she'd ever done was make clothes. Towards the end she had made clothes that were not good. Travesties. Insults. Clothes that had hung awry on Egg and she had told Puppy so. She had given one to the maid. She had needled Puppy, then she had shouted at her. Once she had thrown her cooking at her. Once she had, with infinite sweetness, told Puppy that she smelled. Puppy, with her blotched hair, all yellowed at the front with nicotine, had just stood there. Christ, how she had loathed Puppy!

'Where can I go for the rest of my life?' asked Egg. 'Where can I cover my head? God knows.' She had never given the time of day to God but, 'I want a miracle,' she demanded now. She had never given the time of day to miracles either, but she sighed, opened her eyes and beheld a nun.

The nun was of traditional design. Her old face was oval inside her tight wimple. It beamed at Egg across the aisle of the plane like a Saxon gargoyle on a church porch. On top of the wimple sailed the white headdress like a yacht. No parts of the nun

were apparent except the oval of the face and two
hands busy with beads.

It took Egg a month to get clear of *Psi* and a year
to persuade the Order of Saint Bellavista of Angus to
admit her as postulant for a trial period of twelve
weeks. She had of course made careful researches
until she found an Order that allowed postulants to
cover their ears from the start, before the official
taking of the veil. She moved into the granite
nunnery in granite weather. She took nothing with
her except a pair of scissors hidden round her neck
on a string.

The Scottish nuns were bracing. They frolicked
round the cold wash basins. They had wonderful
complexions. They did not appear to be what Egg
had always thought of as religious. They made noisy,
childish jokes. One or two of them reminded her
very much of scrubbed versions of Puppy.

The first weeks were terrible. She slept in a cell.
She had to roll out of bed and be up through the
smallest hours to say Offices she did not understand
to a God in whom she did not believe. The renunci-
ation of all that she had spent her life fostering, the

beautification and cosseting of the body, left her awash like a corpse in the sea. 'Three months!' she said. 'I'll stick it three days. Then I'll kill myself.'

But all at once she had been there three weeks and was beginning to feel very well. She was starting to be intrigued by the notion of obedience and had decided that she liked the cadence of prayer. The intensely disciplined regime reminded her of austere health farms where she had squandered fortunes in her youth. The map of bells, the hastening feet and the little processions towards plainsong were not so much comfort to her as refuge into certainty, after the vacant clatter of New York.

I haven't a clue what I'm doing, she thought, digging potatoes, mending a sheet, trying with all her might not to imagine that the activity within the veil was less insistent, the hair she had once or twice forgotten to cut at noon less strong. Every morning, as ever, she took herself off to the water closet, her only hiding place, snipped off the tresses, dropped them into the pan, pulled the chain. She watched them swirl easily away in the peaty water. Outside she heard the wild winds in the fir trees and the rattle of a thousand burns.

The food was plain – oats, bannocks, porridge and pale mushy vegetables. Meat only on Sundays. No reading except books of devotion. No cigarettes. No booze. 'Dear Christ,' said Egg, and she put her unpainted fingertips together on either side of her head. The coils did feel lighter.

Not her own legs seemed to take her to the Mother Superior at the end of six weeks. Not her own tongue spoke the words she had never before uttered. 'Mother, I have sinned,' she said. 'I am a non-believer. I came here only out of cowardice from the world because I am almost destroyed by a physical disability.'

'What is it, my child?' asked the Mother Superior of the long pale American woman who never smiled.

Egg was silent for an age. She said, 'I killed my cat.'

'And?' asked the Mother Superior, the yacht upon her head crackling like fire.

'And I have wickedly and for many years tormented and detested my friend, Puppy.'

'You have also killed a puppy?'

'No. She was a woman. I lived with her. I came

to hate her. I don't know why. I couldn't help it. She observed and sniggered but would not quarrel.'

'This doesn't sound like a physical disability.'

'I have hair . . .' said Egg, 'growing out of my ears.'

'So had Beethoven,' said the Mother Superior, 'in large clumps.'

'Mine is long and silky. It grows overnight in swathes. I have to secrete it away. I was the fashion editor of a great magazine and the hair came to destroy me. I am not fanciful. For over two years there has been long golden hair cascading from my ears. And Beethoven was not a woman.'

The Mother Superior pondered. 'You took medical advice of course?'

'It was not possible. I was too afraid. In my world there is little kindness. I came here only because I could cover my ears for ever.'

'You would have been found out. When you took your vows we would have seen your ears when we shaved off your hair.'

'I think it would not have gone so far. I intended to kill myself. This week. This afternoon.'

After a time the Mother Superior said, with

gravity, 'You are penitent, I believe, about your sins with cats and puppies and I do know this: that you are a different woman from the long drink of cold tap-water you were when you came to us. I was beginning to have hopes of you. I am not a priest and therefore I cannot absolve you for making use of us, but I think I can promise you that God has forgiven you.'

Egg felt light. She gave a huge sigh. Tears wetted her cheeks. They felt familiar and delightful, like childhood comfits.

'Maybe I should bless the terrible hair,' she said; 'it has been a martyrdom. But oh, if only I could be cured of it. I am still – I am so sorry – I still cannot bear it.'

'Oh, that,' said the Mother Superior. 'Is that all you want? Forget it. Give me your scissors. The hair has gone.'

'Gone?'

'Undo your veil.'

Egg did, and felt with her fingers the insides of her ears, as hairless, smooth and perfect as the day that she was born.

The Boy who Turned into a Bike

Nancy and Clancy were two little babies who were born on the same day in the same hospital and lived next door to each other for years and years.

Nancy loved Clancy and Clancy loved Nancy, but Clancy loved Nancy more.

Nancy was a rose-and-gold round girl, rather big and sleepy. Clancy was a little rat of a boy, rather small and sharp. When they played doctors and nurses Clancy was always the patient and Nancy the kind, kind nurse. Oh, how he loved his Nancy as she patted and soothed and caressed him.

So they grew up and went to school together, hand in hand, and waited for each other at the end of each school day. At first they were taken and fetched by a parent, usually Nancy's mother because Clancy's mother was always at the Bowlerama or the Bingo or down the pub. Nancy's mother was a great one for being at the Hospice shop or working for Save the Trees or Keeping Britain Tidy, and was never late at the school gate although she worked. She was a curtain-maker, sewing at home.

Well, childhood passed and Nancy changed. Boys began to hang around. Nancy draped herself about the front doorstep, against the doorpost, discussing homework and pop. She was always keen to go dancing. Clancy hadn't grown that much. He spent a lot of time out the front with bits of bikes, oiling and welding and easing and squeezing. He never looked up when Nancy went off to the dancing and she never looked at him. But both of them knew exactly what the other one was up to.

Sometimes even now if there was a crisis on, or around Christmas, Nancy and Clancy met up together alone. They lolled over the telly like husband and wife in Clancy's front room, never needing to speak. Just sometimes, 'How's the bike, then, Clancy?' 'What's your exams like, Nancy?' When Nancy was ill once and couldn't get up – it was a boy, her mother told Clancy's mother: love pains – Clancy went round pretending he wanted a drop of oil and sat in Nancy's kitchen. He never asked for her or how she was, just sat in the kitchen eating Nancy's mother's fairy cakes while she went on about Nancy, and how disappointing she was and what bad company she kept.

But soon there was someone else coming to Nancy's door, not a schoolboy but a man, all flash jeans and earrings. A student. Older than Nancy, with a guitar, and he helped her with her A levels and was besotted. And Nancy, shrugging and yawning, went off with him down the path as Clancy sat at his desk in his front room, studying cycling form. He never needed to do much school work, exams never being anything to him.

Oh Nancy and Clancy – the trouble to come!

Soon there was a serpent calling for rosy-posy Nancy in a car. He would roar up and sit in the road with the radio blasting down the street as he lit up a joint. He didn't trouble to get out of the car, a roofless sports car, bright yellow. Nancy would come running down the path in her mini-frill, black boob-tube and heavy leggings, with her hair done up in barley-sugar bundles and her voice gone silly. And Clancy in his black shell-suit next door, looking polished like a black beetle, lean as a ferret, was all the time on the phone in his front room organising the local cycling club, the Gleaming Wheelers, of which he was founder member, treasurer, secretary and president. The rounder and lovelier and noisier Nancy became, the skinnier, twitchier and less articulate grew Clancy.

Clancy's house began to fill up with trophies from the cycling. First they covered the spaces on the walls of his small bedroom where his bike posters and a few wheels hung. Next they spread over the walls of the front room. Then they lined both sides of the passage and began to climb the stairs. Photographs of Clancy appeared in *Cycling News* and the local papers; and after the night of Nancy's engagement party to the snake in the MG, Clancy won a remarkable hundred in Northants that brought him to the notice of the national press. He couldn't go to Nancy's celebration because of the hundred, the hundred being on a Sunday and Nancy's betrothal the Saturday night before, when Clancy had to have his sleep. Whether he got it or not in his narrow bed next door, with the noise of the pre-nuptial heavy-metal thudding through walls and piercing almost to shattering the closed windows, we shall never know. It was silent enough when Clancy left for his race at 5.00 a.m., picked up by some other ferret-like beings in a minibus with bike racks. Exhaustion oozed from the interior of Nancy's house in that dawn. There were a dozen cars parked all anywhere in the road, some with their doors open, and vomit in the tulips. A cold brisk spring day for Clancy and colder still in Northamptonshire. Up and down the flat, windswept roads, around the great curves of the silver River Nene, went Clancy, in and out of the icy spires of all the famous churches.

Not that Clancy saw any of it. Head down, bottom up, hands steady, legs like pistons up near his ears – all sinew, eyes narrowed – away he went, never looking for an instant at the gauge upon his wrist that checked the heart rate, never deigning to suck from the vitaminised bottle on the tight and glittering oxbow handlebars. He broke a national record that morning (3.31.52) and there was champagne and shouting and it was Clancy-talk at the Northants clubhouse the best part of the night. Some old spindle-shanked veteran, seventy if a day and still doing a good 4.31.00 – a man made of ropework and leather with the fanatical gleaming eye of one who has given his life to the road – this old vet. said he saw the Arc de Triomphe in the tea leaves.

Clancy spoke little, as always. The habit had given him status. Some thought Clancy rather a comic little turn. So silent. No friends. Girls didn't exist. Hardly drank a drop. By trade he was a computer guy, and you can be that without speaking much, but he was a puzzle to his work mates, with whom he never conversed at all. They saw him arriving every day on a different bike, working-out in the Gents and jogging in the lunch break, and after the hundred one or two of them saw his face in the tabloids and were impressed. 'He's nuts,' they said. 'Cycling mad. Nothing else to him. But he's a consistent guy.'

Then something happened. Clancy's mum packed up and went to live with the manager of the Bowl-erama. (His dad had packed up long ago.) She said she was sick of nothing but bikes all over the place and no conversation. 'Clancy's gone funny,' she said. 'See how he gets on without me.' Clancy's mum said she didn't know where Clancy came from and if she hadn't seen for herself the minute he was born she'd have said there'd been a mix-up. That Nancy next door now, there's a smashing girl with a bit of fun about her and her parents nothing but stuffed pudding.

So Clancy's house grew very dirty. From the outside you'd say it was taken over by squatters. Inside it looked like a bike shop, overrun at weekends by little streamlined people, crowds of them, with an eye for nothing but a bike.

Then Nancy's engagement was broken off, though she kept the ring, having paid for it herself, and she slammed the doors a lot and laughed over-loudly and wore don't-care clothes and went off with her parents to the Costa del Sol to get over it, Clancy saying he'd see to the cat and the rubbish and the pipes, it being wintertime. He took custody of the keys from Nancy's father, who slapped him on what passed for his shoulder as he left and said, 'Good lad, Clancy. Why can't she marry you?'

Not that he really meant it, Clancy now being dead eccentric with glittering eyes and twitching hands and an inward-turning heart. But he was much improved in appearance, fit and healthy and weather-beaten and self-confident in his way, people coming to his door for autographs and articles appearing about him in the Sundays entitled *Tour de France 2000?* and *Pride of the Midlands: Cert.* and *Wellborough Wheels Olympic Hope*. All true – but you wouldn't want him in the family. Like a foreigner, he was, inhuman. Dehumanised.

So Clancy took the keys of Nancy's house that fortnight; and every evening, be it ever so late, he'd let himself in and lock the door behind him, and when he'd fed the cat and picked up the junk mail and put it in the box marked Junk Mail he went up to Nancy's bedroom and touched her bed and opened her wardrobe and her chest of drawers and rubbed his little wedge of face into her knickers and bras and her all-over-lace shortie nighties. Once or twice he took off his shoes, turned back the bed cover and got into her brown satin sheets and lay still. He looked at the posters on her walls. Elvis types, rubber-necks, prize-fighters. There was nobody who looked the least like him.

Yet he knew she loved him.

Even when she came back from Spain with a great hairy thing with a paunch at twenty-five and all tattoos and boots, even when she paraded this dream-boy up and down the path next door, even when she introduced him, 'This is Darien, Clancy; we're engaged,' he knew she loved him. Him. Clancy. She flounced about when he just said, 'Hi, Darien,' and went on mending a back sprocket, garage doors behind him open to reveal a laboratory of cyclomatory science. 'Good luck,' he said. The Adonis smirked.

Nancy came round that night, a bit later, on her own. It was the first time she had come round and flopped down on the old sofa since they were kids.

'Can I come in? Heck – you want a few windows open in here. Is this the kitchen? I can't see space for a knife and fork.'

He cleared a stool of cycling magazines and moved the long drape of socks and sweat shirts on the string between the sink and the back door. He went to the sink and started cleaning oil off his hands. 'D'you want a Coke, Nancy?'

They were easygoing as two pensioners, yet they'd not talked for years.

'OK, if you can find one. It's for real this time, Clance. I'm going to do it this time.'

'Why?'

'He's strong. He's nice. He loves me.'

'If that's it, you could have me.'

'Don't be daft.' She looked terrified. She looked appalled. 'Be like marrying your brother.'

'You never had one. I never had a sister. It'd be good.'

'I'm not in your world, Clancy.'

'I don't care about my world, Nance.'

When he said this, standing amid all the paraphernalia – the holy icons on the wall, his lifeblood, his empire – she felt the power of him and ran off back home.

Her mother asked her what was wrong and was she crying and she said no, she'd been over to Clancy and he was pathetic. Just pathetic. And she wasn't having him to the wedding.

'She won't have you to the wedding, Clancy,' said her mother one day when he was disappearing off in his fast car with the bikes in a trailer, sleek like for racehorses. 'I'm ever so sorry, Clancy.'

'I couldn't come anyway,' he said. 'I've got the Nantwich Spa to Scroxton Fifty that day.'

He won it of course. It was his biggest win yet. They wanted to give him a ball. But he came home. Drove himself all the way home that night, got in at three in the morning. Not a sign of a wedding about Nancy's house. It had all been done down the Rotary with red carpets and a toastmaster and white ribbons and everything, a big confetti do. Clancy never looked towards the place as he let himself into his garage, thin, metallic little ferret Clancy, the hero of the world.

And the world never saw him again. Nobody ever saw him again.

Nancy's mother came looking for him in a day or two. She'd heard his telephones ringing and ringing. The place was empty. The cycling people came next. Then the gas man and the electricity and the Council. Then little clutches of people together. Then the press. Then the police. All the world came knocking, but Nancy's mother had seen no sign of him. Had she the keys? No, she had not.

It seemed, though, that Nancy had a key. She'd had one for some time. He'd given it to her when they were both eight and he had been provided with one of his own. Sometimes, between lovers, when Clancy was well away and after his mother's departure,

Nancy would let herself into Clancy's house round the back and wander about in it and clear up a bit where once they used to sit hugging mugs of cocoa or bubbling down their straws into pop, or blowing sprays of biscuit crumbs in each other's face, laughing. She would clean round the bath and basin upstairs and even make his bed and look at all the posters on the wall, all the makes of bike. Examine all the trophies.

She would relive the one occasion when he had come in unexpectedly and found her there, a day when he'd not done very well in a Huntingdon–Lincoln Seventy-five and he was dejected. And sweaty. He had stood numb and she had taken him in her arms and they had lain together on the bed wrapped and lapped, soft and kind, warm and true, as if for ever. They never knew which one of them it was who had pulled away.

Clancy's mother came back after Clancy disappeared. She had been off with a pop group half her age and was into holistic medicine and E-tabs and seemed uncertain who Clancy had been. The police were stumped, the Sally Army too, and there was a lot of publicity and talk of murder by jealous competitors, though this is scarcely the way of the cycling world.

The house was sold, Clancy's mother needing money, and in the garage into which Clancy had last stepped was found, standing among his other bicycles, one of the most exquisite crafting: under twenty-five ounces, light enough to lift by a finger, equipped with every known and unknown development of bicycle wizardry.

Nancy, when she saw it, knew that it was Clancy. 'Can I have it?' she asked.

'What do you want with a bike?' asked his mother. 'I'm the one that should have it. It's all I'll have to remember him by. I'll take a thousand pounds.'

'Done,' said Nancy, and wheeled it away.

It lived at home with her, at first in the *en-suite* garage of the detached house in Park Drive, and after that, in its Jamaican-style extension; then, in the built-on cedar-wood conservatory. But this she found too cold for it in winter, even with rugs and blankets, so it came into the kitchen and stood by the Aga and every time she passed it she stroked it. When she took it up into their bedroom, however, her husband threatened to leave her. Once, when, during the menopause, she took it into her bed, he did leave her.

He came back, though. He had seen doctors about her and had counsellors come round to talk to her. These people spoke of mania and she threw a chair at them and climbed passionately on top of Clancy and rode away.

Away and away she rode on the long firm saddle, up and down, up and down the hills. The hills flew from her as she rode. She rode like Juliet fleeing towards her tomb, and 'Clancy, Clancy, Clancy' yearned her heart.

The Pillow Goose

There were two sisters, Maude and Angela, who lived on the Thanet marshes in a cottage left to them by their great-grandmother. They were craft workers in metals, wool and dried flowering things and they were as green as grass.

They would eat no meat, nor anything from a dairy; their shoes were made of plastic and they fainted at the sight of furs. They took all their empty bottles and tins and their waste paper to the tip every Sunday morning at eight o'clock prompt, like Communion, and put everything carefully down the right holes.

The sisters had no husbands but many lovers and because they did not believe in contraception except by the phases of the moon there were many babies born in the cottage over the years, and these all grew up and went away; and the sisters took life lightly as the leaves grow on the tree and as they grew older sang as happily as ever at the loom and

forge and dyeing-tub, bashing out the metals for
their quaint and fairly unsaleable jewellery, eating
home-made bread, baked more or less evenly, in
their twig-burning stove, washing their long and
beautiful hair in the purest non-animal soaps or with
some of their great-grandmother's herbal mixtures
and drying it under the flowering trees of their little
orchard.

When lovers had grown scarce and their hair was
becoming grey there came one day to the cottage
the most enchanting Ethiopian gypsy, and the sisters
were happy. When he left them after several days,
secretly one morning at dawn, they found on the
rough old kitchen table propped up with a log
the gift of a sort of hay-box and inside it two
beautiful goose eggs. Maude and Angela wept at the
gypsy's going, laughed at the strange present and
shoved it under the table. They went on with their
work, each with her own sweet thoughts about the
gypsy's visit.

Out from the eggs hatched two untidy-looking
goslings and the sisters looked up in one of their
grandmother's useful books in the garret some rules
about rearing them. They installed them in an old

henhouse, where they became magnificent white geese.

Quite soon there were more eggs, which in turn became scruffy goslings and then more white geese. The sisters grew to love all the geese and the flock increased. In no time at all there was a great gaggle of the most dazzling and noble birds moving with stately tread in little troupes among the cherry trees, beaks left, beaks right, cackle, cackle, cackle. They seemed whiter and more perfect than any known geese. Had each worn on the top of its silken head a miniature crown like in the ballet *Swan Lake* you would only have thought, How very appropriate.

Word went round, as it does, about these geese in the Thanet marshes. Somehow they became known as 'the Ethiopian Royal Geese', and of course everyone knows that Ethiopian pillow down has been treasured for a millennium at least. One small bolster will cost you hundreds of pounds. The heads of royalty have lain on such things since Tamburlaine came crashing through Asia. King Arthur gave them as prizes for knightly behaviour all round the round table, and the Pharaohs were provided with stacks of them in the Pyramids to comfort them into the next world.

Dreams that arise from such pillows are most disturbing and delicious and the sisters, who had always been poor, came to understand that they were now in charge of a fortune.

But they did not believe in the slaughter of animals, and geese, ever famous for clearing up rubbish, for their comic beauty, for their filthy temper and for saving Rome, are best of all known for being creatures for the pot and for delicious horrors like *pâté de foie gras*. And the plucking of the famous down, so light and soft that it seems caught from the very air, like clouds of dandelion fluff, down that has to be escorted to the pillow-makers by special messengers armed with machine guns and mortars to places of special safety – this down can only be obtained after the goose is dead.

Now the sisters were not greatly frightened about owning the miraculous brood, for it is hard to steal geese. They are fearsome as the rhinoceros and faster, and they have powers that can tell the approach of a robber at half a mile. What did agitate the sisters as the flock grew were the endless visits of the pillow-makers of the world to discuss lucrative deals. They were also troubled by the enormous fecundity of the geese, who were now standing shoulder to shoulder (if geese have shoulders) in the orchard, and soon spread across the little garden, tight as the Royal Enclosure at Ascot, in the heavily fenced paddock. Every old shed, the rickety barn, the old earth closet, the tumbledown cow-house long unused, the coal-hole, the wood store and, at length, the scullery, the parlour and the spare bedroom were filled with geese, and from the air the land surrounding the cottage looked as if it was in the grip of a deep snowstorm. The raucous music of the geese could be heard far across the marshes, disturbing the slumbers of sailors out in the English Channel. The smell of the geese, and the depth of their excreta (which even in the Ethiopian Royal Goose resembles bundles of large rotting cigars), was causing concern to the workers in the gentler fumes of the Richborough power-station. In Canterbury Cathedral the clergy were wearing face masks for Evensong. Animal rights groups were vociferous about the overcrowded conditions and although the sisters were paid-up card-carrying members of these organisations they were spared nothing by their own kind, who now stood round the cottage regularly, chanting and waving banners.

The girls would not sell or give away any of the geese, of course, for how can you ever trust anyone not to make an easy, if bloodstained, fortune?

So there had to be found a way to limit the breeding powers of the geese without contraception and to pluck their down without causing pain; and this seemed quite impossible until one day Maude thought of the idea of using temporary anaesthetic before plucking, after which the creatures might be wrapped in warm coats until their feathers grew again.

Maude and Angela presented themselves then to various distinguished veterinarians of the day, who were each and all totally unsympathetic to their ideas. Next they sat in the cottage in deep thought, until Angela said, 'Perhaps our great-grandmother, who was known for her herbal simples, might be of some help.'

So they ransacked the shelves in the garret again and came upon a bottle thick with cobwebs labelled 'For the temporary sterilisation and anaesthetising of geese for the purpose of de-downing'.

Then Maude and Angela set about making a woollen garment like a baby's romper-suit, with holes for legs and slits for wings and aperture facilities for private and egg-laying parts, and good strong press-studs down the breast and along the undercarriage. They knitted hundreds of these suits in strong white wool, then scattered about half the contents of the cobwebby bottle in the goose mash. There was an old, old, faded label on the bottle but no directions about the strength of the contents, which turned out to be a thick, bluish-black liquid like an old-peculiar treacle.

The next morning every goose in the goosery was lying on its back with its great yellow feet in the air and its black eyes shut. The sisters took them two by two and with several friends of their own ilk (and not prone to sneezing) they settled themselves in the parlour of the cottage and plucked all day and all night. Gently they lifted the geese from the sheds and the coal-hole and the barn and the outside loo and the scullery and the spare bedroom and gently they replaced them, all garbed in their comfortable knitting. From a distance they still looked simply like white geese.

And in the cottage the pluckers sat for all the world as if they were out of the world; inside a luminous airy summer cloud.

Now the sisters had to wait and see. About luncheon time the feet of the geese began to twitch, the necks of the geese began to turn this way and that in their usual stiff fashion, the fierce black eyes of the geese began to open and the outraged, ill-tempered, arrogant gobble of the geese began to gobble.

And Maude and Angela went to London in a hired van and sold the down for a fortune, keeping back just enough for a pillow each for themselves. Most of the fortune they immediately gave away to good causes. It is said that no finer goose down has ever been known in the history of the world.

The sisters now looked after the flock very kindly. The geese seemed happy in their knitted coats, perfectly well and perhaps pleased at their rest from egg-laying. Some died, but only in the natural way of things and from old age. A fox got one – its knitted coat, two webbed feet and a beak were found beside the boundary fence, and this saddened the sisters and they tried hard not to rejoice when the fox was found lying dead with a blue-black tinge to its face: for all animals act only according to their nature and death comes to us all.

What was more troubling to the sisters was that the white woollen coats of the geese were now growing filthy. They had sagged or shrunk with the weather, become studded with burrs and prickles and twigs, and the geese had begun to pull and tear at them with their beaks and to stand about in silent humiliation.

One morning Maude came in from taking the geese their mash, puzzled. 'Come and see,' she said.

'What?' asked Angela.

'Do you not see something strange?'

Angela looked at the flock in their dirty woollies under the polished fruits of the cherry trees. She said, 'They seem to be faintly coloured, somehow, under the wool.'

They had a go at catching a few to see what was going on beneath, but the geese would have none of it. They hissed and spat and lunged at Maude and Angela. Their eyes were sad and wild.

The sisters then ransacked the garret to see if

there were any bottles to do with the rehabilitation of un-downed geese, but there were none. They tried again to read the label of the cobwebby bottle. No go. And the bottle now was empty. The blue treacle had vanished.

Maude and Angela were distraught. The geese had begun to look, quite suddenly, like neglected, dirty toddlers trailing woollen rompers, and they fixed the sisters with daemonic stares and would not let them near. They began to wilt and pine and sink to the ground like little heaps of washing. At the gate of the cottage the animal rights people chanted, and about the world the pillow-makers would not cease their clamouring for more down.

Then a boy came knocking at the door, a dark boy with sparkling eyes and a cross face who said his name was Scratch.

'I think I know you,' said Angela.

'You should do,' he said. 'I'm your son.'

'Darling,' said Angela. 'My own.'

'Angel,' said Maude. 'My treasure.'

'I don't know which of you I belong to,' said Scratch; 'I never did. It was a messy life, this place, but I suppose I love you and your high notions and

I've come to save you,' and he sat all night up a tree in the orchard, playing his flute. (He had to sit up a tree because the grass was disgusting.) And all through the night hours the geese listened and grew calm, and Angela and Maude sat in the parlour trying to remember details of old times and murmuring that there must some years ago have been another and musical Ethiopian. And they fell asleep in their chairs.

In the morning the flute was silent and the boy had gone. Tearfully, Maude and Angela looked for him. There was a great silence in the goosery: none of the usual clamour of geese getting ready to attack the day. The sisters opened doors and goose flaps and found that during the night the ragged woollen garments had been slipped like the old dull skins of snakes, and there streamed out across the orchard and paddock a silent flock all the colours of the rainbow from psychedelic green to the most sinister indigo. The pink ones looked like giant toilet rolls squatting in the sedge.

The press arrived *en masse*. The cottage made the national news. The RSPCA sent representatives from head office. Many members of the animal rights roups had apoplexy. Local foxes blanched and fled.

Later that day every laying goose in the place dropped a rainbow-coloured egg and, along with the rest of the flock, lay down and died. All the eggs (except perhaps one or two that Scratch had acquired sometime in the dawn and made off with in a little hay-box) were addled from the start; they rolled away into the grass of the orchard, where the trees all grew cankers and wilted and never fruited more. The two sisters, Angela and Maude, packed their bags and disappeared, each with her one down pillow under her arm. It is thought they went to Abyssinia.

Very occasionally since then a Thanet twitcher on the mud flats has glimpsed a most astonishing bird. It is like a jewel shining on the dun fields, a gleam like a Roman standard blowing among the stones of Richborough Castle, where the centurions are said to have first arrived in Britain from Alexandria with the seeds of the pink valerian on their boots. The valerian still flowers there like a weed, a rather crude and ugly pink along the

Thanet lanes. But the story of its origin is of course ridiculous.

Unlike that of the ghostly Rainbow Pillow-Goose of Thanet. He exists, all right. He is a wonder and a warning to the world.

Two Hauntings

Soul Mates

When Francis Phipps retired, he and his wife, Patricia, took a week's holiday on the Isles of Scilly. They were a prudent pair and had booked the best room in the hotel the previous summer. It had always been summer when they holidayed on the Scillies long ago, with their young children, all now successfully scattered about the world.

Patricia Phipps had been uncertain about this return visit (and the long motorway journey *à deux*). She thought it might be sad. But Francis said, What nonsense! How delightful to be going back again with enough money for a luxurious hotel instead of the sandy-floored pub with its one bathroom.

'We shall take plenty of books,' he said. 'The daffodils will be at their best. We shall walk. The food should be marvellous and with luck there'll be very few people.'

But it was cold. Their room was glorious, but stood at the end of several blustery corridors and three of its walls were windows on to the sea. The sea sucked and roared and ground and slapped against the very foundations of the single-storey hotel and seemed, in some way, to tower over them in their beds. Beyond the spraying breakers they could see the shine and dazzle of it to the far horizon. The Phippses seemed to swing with the sea when they closed their eyes.

Each day they walked in the salty wind, along lanes lined with chill, flattened daffodils that ran in trickles and eddies and torrents. Their shouting yellow was round every red boulder, every stiff, black escallonia hedge.

After luncheon they slept. After dinner they read their books. It was a hotel of great discretion and, although always full, seemed empty. There were a few couples of the Phippses' age, a tense little writer person with frizzy, iron-grey hair, a desolate-looking woman in a wonderful beaded dress of bright-blue wool, and a Yorkshire couple, she fat and amiable, he gaunt and glum. The wife smiled eagerly across the restaurant at the Phippses.

'Bit ominous, the wife,' said Francis. 'She looks as if she might *divulge*.'

'We can keep her at bay,' said Patricia.

Patricia was tired. The past few months of small, decorous but nevertheless emotional retirement parties for Francis had drained them both. Since the university, where they had met forty years ago, Francis had served his country and his Department and Pat had served him. Her achievement had been to create his setting, which was a tranquil house in Dulwich and dignified hospitality. In its long green garden there hung a pink hammock between a walnut tree and a pear.

Two nights before the end of their holiday, Pat felt a great longing to be back in this garden, and Francis, at the same moment, holding the door for her to pass into the long corridors *en route* for dinner, said, 'I'd say that a week was about long enough here, Patricia. Wouldn't you?'

There was a slight easing-up, though, tonight in the dining-room. Somebody was laughing softly as they went in, and the grizzled novelist, wearing a black velvet suit, was drinking her coffee at the table of the wronged woman in the couture dress. The Yorkshire wife, rosy from the weather, was now looking hungrier than ever for conversation, and at last called shamelessly across from her table to the Phippses that her holiday was nearly over, and was theirs? She had to be back in Boroughbridge on Saturday, for her results.

'Oh,' said Pat. 'Examination results?'

'Yes, I'm afraid so. I've had a medical examination. We're rather wondering What They Will Have Found.'

Francis picked up his napkin and Pat picked up the menu. As she looked up from it, she met the glance of one of the other couples, sitting across from them, rather in the shadow of the staircase. The woman smiled at her like a sister. Pat thought for a second that she was looking in a glass.

When the pair left their table, the man came over and smiled at Francis. 'Good evening.'

'Good evening.'

The woman said to Patricia, 'I'm afraid things tend to get rather chatty by Thursday. Beware of people with operations!'

Later the four found themselves together in the television room, waiting for the News, and the other man ('Phillips – Jocelyn Phillips. My wife – Evelyn') said that nowadays he hated the News.

'We sit in horror,' said Francis. 'We fear for our young.'

'You sound exactly like Jocelyn,' said the wife. 'Now – let me guess. You are at the Bar? A judge?'

'A civil servant. I have just retired.'

'Me, too,' said Phillips. 'Foreign Office. I went last year.'

The men bought brandy for each other and the women drank liqueurs. Conversation flowered. They were like old friends.

The next day they all walked together to the tropical gardens and Evelyn and Pat found a mutual interest in lilies. Automatically the four met up again after dinner, and at bedtime Jocelyn Phillips said how much they had enjoyed the day. Francis, for years considered to be the coldest of fish, said, 'It has been *delightful* to meet you.'

Coming over to the Phippses' table at breakfast next day, Evelyn said, 'Now – look. I do hope you don't think us *quite* extraordinary, but we wondered if you'd come and stay with us tonight, on your way home? We're hardly off your route and it would break up the awful motorway journey a bit.'

Francis, standing, clutching his napkin, said, 'But how *very* kind.'

'Excellent idea,' Jocelyn called across.

At the reception desk, as they paid their bills, all four turned to one another.

'D'you know—' said Francis. 'If you really mean it—?'

'Of *course* we do. Give us an hour's start to make things ready.'

'Well, this is *most* friendly . . . Pat—?'

'But I should love to.'

Address and directions given, everybody climbed into the helicopter for the mainland and their parked cars. Pat was surprised to see the woman in the couture dress and the writer saying affectionate goodbyes to the Yorkshire couple. She and Francis waved off the Phillipses and went to the nearby village for coffee and to look for a potted plant to take as a present.

'What an extraordinary thing we're doing,' she said. 'Whatever would the children say? They may be *anyone*. Serial killers. Somehow – did you think they looked rather . . . cold, when they went off? Remote?'

'Nonsense,' he said. 'They're exactly like us. It's great luck. You hardly ever meet your own sort these days.'

Pat thought of the novelist and the rich woman and the Yorkshire pair. None of them had said goodbye to her. She felt suddenly miserable. Cut off.

Miles further on, deep into Devonshire, Francis said at last, 'Oh, well . . . It *is* a slight risk, I suppose. "Never take up with people you meet on holiday", and so on. But we've not met people we've felt so at home with for years. We must be almost at their turning, are we not?'

The motorway exit was just ahead and he swung towards it much too fast. As always she said, 'I hate the way you do that. You should let me drive.' Usually he didn't answer, but today he said, 'Wrist a bit wonky. Traffic's much worse these days. I must say I don't enjoy driving any more. Train next time.'

They reached the A-road, then the roundabout for the byroad, and then – yes, here it was – the turning for the house (no signpost) and the little lane.

The lane was long. It turned at sharp angles, like the corridors at the hotel. It narrowed and became unkempt. Grass grew down a central ridge. Hedges gave way to a long, metal field-fence and through it could be seen a red-brick house with lattice windows, standing well back from the road and surrounded by grass. Its front and back doors were standing wide open so that you could see down a flagstoned passage to more green fields behind.

'Is it genuine?' asked Pat. 'Or pseudo-Tudo?'

'Can't tell,' he said. 'Very cunning if it's pseudo.'

They stepped from the car into total silence. Crocuses along the front of the house looked like flowers painted on a calendar.

'It's empty,' she said. 'They can't have arrived.'

'It can't be,' said Francis: 'the doors are open.' He knocked. 'Hello there? Hello?'

Not liking to walk in, they went round the side of the house to the back. A barn. A double garage. A shed or stable far across the field. No life.

'Maybe it's the wrong house,' said Francis. '*Hello?*'

Suddenly, there were the Phillipses far away beside the shed, standing quite still. And then, as if a pause-button had been released, they began to move forward over the grass. They looked graver sort of people than those in the hotel.

But this passed at once. The Phippses were welcomed warmly and the men went off to get the luggage from the car. Evelyn took Pat into the house and the green spring day went in with them. There were books everywhere, an open log fire, photographs of exemplary children on a grand piano, a nice old overhead clothes-airer on the ceiling of the red-and-yellow tiled kitchen.

'I feel I've known this house all my life,' said Pat. 'It's like my old home.'

'The four of us are so alike,' said Evelyn. 'Have you noticed that we all have androgynous names?'

Pat looked away and said she hoped that Evelyn didn't think that she and Francis were androgynous.

Evelyn laughed brightly and said she had really meant *genderless*. 'All our names are *genderless*. It's so good to be genderless now.'

'What did you do as a young woman, Pat?' she asked later, washing salad in cold water.

'Well, nothing, I suppose. After I left Oxford.'

Evelyn, amazed, cried, 'But neither did I! I married straight from Cambridge. I thought there was nobody left like us.'

Dinner was perfect. Duck and green peas and a crème brulée.

'But however did you spirit it all up in an hour?' asked Francis.

Jocelyn produced a second bottle of superb wine.

Their bedroom was old-rose chintz and a four-poster. There were flowers, and hot-water bottles.

'It is *heaven!*' said Pat. She wondered whether to kiss Evelyn's cheek, or even Jocelyn's. She let it go.

Francis, flushed with duck and claret, said, 'Yes. Heaven.' He paused. 'The hotel was good,' he said, 'but we were restless there. It was the sea.'

'Ah, the sea,' said Jocelyn Phillips.

'We shall sleep tonight,' said Pat. '*Utterly.*'

And they did sleep. They slept until nearly ten o'clock the following morning, and could not believe it.

They awoke to silence.

'My God,' said Francis, 'we'd better get on if we're to be home before we hit the rush hour. Better miss a bath.'

'Hello?' Pat called on the stairs. In the hall. 'We're thoroughly ashamed of ourselves. Hello?'

No sound.

They looked in kitchen, dining-room, drawing-room, study. There was no trace of last night's dinner or sign of today's breakfast. Front and back doors stood open.

'D'you think we could look in the bedrooms?'

There was nobody there.

In the Phillipes' bedroom not a thing was out of place. No clothes over chairs, no holiday unpacking, not a hair in a comb. The beds were carefully made up.

The Phippses went outside. Barn, garage and shed watched them, but there was nobody. Pat pointed. 'Was that there last night?' Across the garden a large, lazy pink hammock was slung between trees.

'Well, look here,' Francis said, 'we have to go. This is ridiculous. I'll leave a note. It's very upsetting.'

He wrote the note and propped it against the kitchen telephone, where the red message-light flashed.

'D'you think we should press it?' he said.

'No,' she said. 'No. Don't,' and grabbed his arm.

'Why not?'

'*No!*'

They closed the back door and the front door. It was some sort of a gesture. It had to be done. They drove away down the drive.

'I don't like doing this,' he said. 'I don't like it at all. I should have pressed that button. Well . . . we'll ring them up tonight. Naturally—'

'I'm not sure,' she said. 'I'm not sure I want to. I'm not sure we shall be able to. Oh, Francis, I'm not sure we'll get home.'

He took her hand and held it as he drove. Steering one-handed along the lane beside the wire fence, they both looked together at the house as they passed it by.

The front door and the back stood wide open again. They could see clearly to the green fields beyond.

The Green Man
An Eternity

The Green Man is no enemy of Christ.
Ronald Blythe

1 The Green Man

The Green Man stood in the fields. In the darkness of winter he was only a shadow.

People going to the tip to throw away their Christmas trees noticed the shadow as their cars sped down the lanes. 'That shadow,' they said. 'Over there.'

Later, in January, the shadow looked like a stump or a post. 'Tree struck by lightning over there,' they said as they rushed along to work at the power-station across the fields. 'Unsightly-looking thing.' If they were local people who had lived here some time they said, 'Look, there's that stump thing again.

Strange how you never seem to notice until it's back.'

When blowy March came and the days seemed to lighten over the dunes, and you could hear the sea tossing and see it spouting up, people on their way to early holidays across the water and beyond the Alps would say, 'Well, someone's been planting seeds. There's a scarecrow. Spring will likely come.'

For the Green Man would now be standing with arms astretch and head askew and all his tatters flying, blustering grey and black and dun against the dun fields and the grey sky and the black thorn-bushes. There was beginning to be something rakish and reckless now about the Green Man.

Then in April the Green Man stood forth in cold sunshine, his hands folded over the top of his hoe and his chin on his hands, and in the dawn light of Eastertime people talking or jogging or riding by, eating things and laughing, quarrelling, shouting and singing, saw him there clearly, and bright green.

His old black clothes looked green and his winter skin looked bronze-green like a Malay's. His eyes were amber-green and one minute you saw him, and the next minute you didn't.

'Did you see that Man!?'

'What man?'

'That Man over there in that field. No – too late. It's gone now. Like a statue. Gold. No, green.'

'It must be advertising something.'

'Did you see that *man*?' the children cried, looking backwards from car windows, and the grown-ups went on talking or didn't bother to answer.

The old country people would say, 'Maybe it's the Green Man.'

'What's the Green Man?'

'Nobody knows. He's some man that's always been around here. I used to see him when I was little. I'd have thought he'd be dead by now.'

'The Green Man?' the granny would say. Then: 'Never! It couldn't be. I used to see the Green Man when I was a child and, even then, there was talk of him being as old as Time. He had other names, too. He lived hereabouts somewhere.'

Then a leery, queery old voice from somebody wrapped up in the back of the car among the babies

– it would be something after the nature of a great-grandfather – would say, 'I seed the Green Man wunst when I were in me bassinette in petticoats. We called him Green Man or mebbe Wildman. And my old pa, he said his old pa seed the Wild Green Man one day. It was the day my old greaty-greaty-grandpop went marching long this lane in his cherry-coloured coat, to the field of Waterloo.'

'The only Green Man I know', the Dad would say as he drove the car, far too fast, round corners of the lane that, after all, were once the right-angled bends round the fields, 'is a pub,' and he'd rush them along towards the motorway that joined up with the Channel Tunnel or the ferry.

'If it was the Green Man,' the children would some-times say as they stood on the deck of the ferry and looked back at the sparkling white cliffs with their grass-green icing, 'however *old* can he be? He could be a hundred.'

Nobody knew.

And nobody knows.

Under different names the Green Man may be a

thousand years old. Or ten thousand. But his eyes are young and bright and by the time it's midsummer he is looking dangerously attractive and permanent. He has never had a grey hair in his head. In his sea-green eyes of July is a far-away magical gaze, if you can get near enough to see it. But it is hard to get near. Now you see him, now you don't. The field is empty and you'll be lucky to catch a glimmer of a face between branches, down the coppice. Did you see a figure at work with a bill-hook by the blackthorn in white bloom? Maybe you didn't.

Or he may pass you silently on the dyke above, when you're fishing the field drains. In the warm dusk at the top of summer he is like the nightingale and gone for deep woodland places. At dawn he is like the skylark, a speck on the blue sky.

Do not imagine that the Green Man is soft and gentle on his land. For all his stillness he is given to rages. He likes to observe and see things right.

'Get off your backsides,' he has been known to roar. 'Keep to your element.' He shouts this at seed-time and harvest, yells at those – there aren't many – who know him well.

Sadie and Patsy and Billy, the next-farm children, know him well, and they hang around him and huggle his legs and ankles. They tickle the bare place between his boots and his trouser bottoms, they tease him with teazles.

'Get off your backsides and out of this drill,' yells the Green Man at these babies. 'This drill!' he yells.

A drill is a long straight furrow in the earth into which the seeds are trickled and then covered up. The Green Man makes thousands of drills across the earth until it looks like corduroy cloth. The seeds grow and turn into one thing or another. They whiten with tendrilly peas, they turn green-gold with barley. Barley whiskers are the colour of a princess's hair.

'Get off my *land*,' bellows the Green Man as he sees the cat coming, on tiptoe, paddling and playing, chewing at the barley stalks in the heat. 'Get off my *back*,' he thunders next, as the cat comes lapping and weaving and purring and winding around him, growling like a motor, springing up, all claws, to land like needles on the Green Man's shoulders and even his head. Very bad language follows then. 'Get off, you filthy scat-scumfish cat. Each to his *element.*'

The cat drops off the Green Man and lies on its back and shows the Green Man its fluffy white stomach and grins up at him. All animals are interested in the Green Man, but he by no means treats them like pets. And he doesn't treat people like pets.

As the year passes, the Green Man keeps away from people more and more. In high summer, deep in the trees he watches, very stiff and silent.

He will watch in secret. You can see carvings of him in churches like this. Watching you. It has always been so. He has always been there. Sometimes he is a leaf-mask on a frieze. Sometimes he looks like leaves only.

2 The Green Man Mounts a Mouse Hunt

The Green Man keeps a house for comfort, but he's seldom inside it. He has had wives in his time, maybe hundreds, and they have tried to care for it. One wife cannot have been long-since, for he has twelve sons and four daughters living, very sturdy. Of course they may be much older than they look.

The twelve sons are scattered about the world, as sons tend to be, but the four daughters visit regularly, as daughters are more likely to do. The house is like a lark's nest lying low in the fields. The doors and the windows of the house are always open until the daughters close them. They visit, bringing bread and milk and lamb chops and short-bread, cleaning fluids, dishcloths and porridge. They flick about with feather dusters and say, 'This place gets no better. Lord, how it smells of mice!' They go looking for their father in the flicker of the poplars and down the marsh and across the fields near the sea.

The mice are not in the house at all on these occasions. Mice can smell daughters as daughters can smell mice. When they hear the daughters' cars arriving, their noses twitch and they're off into the bushes.

But when the daughters have gone away again, the mice creep greedily back.

The mice are fieldmice, but this is a misnomer. They should be called pantrymice or cupboardmice or pocketmice. They run in the Green Man's chests of drawers and armoires, in his bags of meal and flour. They run among the dishcloths and in the Green Man's little-used blanket. They lie, fat and lazy, in the fold of his folded deck-chair. They nestle in his boots and nest in his woollen cardigan and in the pocket of the mackintosh that hangs on the back of the kitchen door.

Do not imagine that the Green Man is a saint to these mice.

The weather one spring was cruelly sharp and perhaps the Green Man was feeling the weight of his two or three thousand years. He was using his house for sleeping every night. He was even occasionally lighting his dangerous paraffin stove which lit with a pop and a blob.

One day he lay down on his couch in the daytime, sneezing, with his cushion and his rug. He felt heavy with years and he coughed as he slept. And awoke to the mice running across his face like rain. He felt them running about in his blanket and snuffling at his toes. There was activity in his green-gold hair. With a roar he lit the lamp and found a mouse making off with a green curl to her nest in his boot.

'This must end!' cried the Green Man. 'The time has come. Each to his *element*.' And the next day he set off down the lane with his cheque-book and confronted the corn chandler's in the High Street of the nearest market town. The corn chandler's stands between the supermarket and the popso-bar, but it does a good trade.

How very strange the Green Man looked, holding out his cheque-book, demanding a writing implement. 'Mouse poison,' cried the Green Man: 'a quantity.'

Someone ran out into the yard and called in others. 'There's a right one here.'

'Who is it? What is it? Where's it from? Is it human? Why's it green?'

The old pale-faced corn chandler sat by the fire in the back of the office. 'It'll be the Green Man,' he said.

'Is it the Council? Is it political? Is it trouble?'

'It's the Green Man.'

'He's for killing mice. He's no *green* man. Is he out of a fairground?'

'Don't thwart him,' said the corn chandler. 'Don't thwart the Green Man,' he said, poking the fire.

The Green Man walked back along the ice-rutted lanes and the cold air puffed from his mouth like a dragon. 'Mice,' he muttered, 'mice. Each to his element.'

When he reached home he called, 'This is to fettle you. Back to your fields,' and he lifted the lid of the flour kist and saw fat, snoring, distended mice from weeks back lying like drunken skiers in the snow. They looked comfortable and in bliss.

These were the ones who were still sleeping and hadn't realised yet that the more flour they ate, the less likely they would be to get out. There were a number of dead ones. The Green Man tipped the whole brigade out into the grass. The ones who could still snore woke up and made off, looking foolish.

The foolish look of the released mice amused the Green Man, and he liked them after all as they ran away. Then he looked with shame at the mouse poison in the great drum he had bought from the corn chandler. Where to put it for safety until he could take it back and swap it for seed?

He put the drum inside the flour crock for the moment and went off to the fields, where he stood planning the year in the March weather.

The Green Man can make mistakes, for he is a man.

3 The Green Man Goes to the Seaside

Usually the Green Man keeps away from the ocean. He likes the drains and dykes and goits and runnels that water his land and the green rushes that spike them. He watches the arrows of the water voles, the mirror the water makes for sailing swans or flying geese. The eyes of these creatures watch the Green Man as he passes. None of them comments.

But beyond the dykes and the marsh is the sea, which is not the natural element of the Green Man. Sometimes when a sheep strays to the strand he has to go down there looking for it, but the sea feels hostile and full of anachronisms.

Most of all the Green Man detests mermaids.

Whenever he is forced to go anywhere near the sea he keeps his eyes off the rocks.

'Yoo-hoo, coo-eee,' call the mermaids, giggling and twiddling their golden ringlets through their fingers. 'Who can't swim, then, Lover-boy?' Two of the mermaids are called Ermentrude and Cayley.

'Coo-eee, Green Man, you don't dare touch us.'

'Half-and-halves,' mutters the Green Man. 'No sense of their element.' He watches his dog, and only his dog. His dog is flurrying the sheep home. 'Neither wet nor dry,' snarls the Green Man. 'Beyond my understanding.'

But one day the mermaids are so provocative and insolent that the Green Man turns and walks right into the sea.

Ermentrude and Cayley are so surprised they forget to slither away, and sit with their pouty little mouths each in an oh! They throw up their hands, ooh la! Ermentrude's golden comb decorated with limpets falls into the sea.

The Green Man seizes the two mermaids, one under each arm. Abandoning the sheep and his dog, he marches back over the dry land, leaving marsh and dykes and drains behind him. Two gliding swans behold him from the water and raise their eyebrows.

'Help, help,' squeak the percussive mermaids and wave their little white arms out front, their tails wagging, slap, slap, behind.

The Green Man goes into his house and tucks both mermaids under one arm for a moment while he fills up the bath-tub from the keg. Then he slings the pair of them in.

'Sit there,' he says, 'till I think what to do with you. Each to his element. Find what it is.'

He goes off to dig his potatoes.

'He's coming back again,' say the water voles. They had caught sight of his retreating figure and thought he had been very successfully fishing.

'He's coming back again,' says the next-door farmer (Jackson), who is the grandson of Sadie-long-ago. He has seen the Green Man pass, but only from the front. 'He's abducting women now,' he says. 'This might be nasty.'

Jackson goes into the Green Man's house and sees two girls' heads looking over the edge of the bath-tub. When they see the next-door farmer they begin to giggle and sing, so that he says, 'Well! So you were willing, were you? I'm disgusted,' and slams off.

The water voles tell it all to some seagulls. Seagulls think they are nobody's fool. They take nothing on trust. They fly to the bathroom window and look in. Twirling fishtails whirlpool the water. 'Couple of fish,' they report. 'No worries.'

The four daughters of the Green Man happen to be visiting that day and they are surprised to see the mermaids in the bath-tub. By this time the mermaids are growing tetchy and needing salt.

'There'll be big damages for this,' screeches Ermentrude.

'It's a scandal,' squawks Cayley. 'It's a threat to the environment. Haphazard. Erratic. He's a danger to the community. *Green* Man, my tail!'

The daughters found a small tin hip-bath, filled it with tank water and took the mermaids, one at a time, back to the sea. The tide had gone out and they had a long walk. Each mermaid delivered a separate scolding all the way, protesting that it was dangerous for them to be separated, and similar rubbish.

'Shut up,' said the daughters, 'or we'll drop you in the shallows and you'll have to wriggle off like eels in an ungainly way.'

'Stuff you all,' said the mermaids as they each glided quickly into the deep.

The daughters noticed the Green Man digging his potatoes as, carrying the empty hip-bath, they returned from the sea for the second time and they were so cross with him that they passed him by without speaking. When they were back in the house, though, they made tea and caught each other's glance and couldn't stop laughing.

'You should have sliced them in half,' said the Green Man coming in; 'I was thinking of it. Mermaid-tail fillet is a little-known delicacy, too sensible a concept for fairy tale.'

'It *is* a fairy tail,' said the most amusing of the daughters, but all the others – and the Green Man – groaned.

'And *you* thought to be a conservationist!' said the eldest daughter.

'I don't know why,' said the Green Man. 'Most of it's guesswork. Folklorists. Folk-laureates.' (Now the amusing daughter groaned.) 'Each to his element,' said the Green Man. 'No messing.'

The mermaids were no bother to the Green Man after this. Ermentrude's golden comb with the limpets was washed up at Ramsgate and sold at a boot fair.

4 The Green Man Goes with the Devil to the Moon

It was one evening in early summer when the Green Man met the Devil under an apple tree in the orchard.

'I'd heard you favoured fruit,' said the Green Man, offering him a Worcester Pearmain.

'Good evening,' said the Devil, with a charming, quizzical look; 'I'd been hoping we'd meet.'

The Green Man looked hard at the Devil and thought, *But this must be a looking-glass. He is just like me.*

The Green Man walked all round the apple tree and examined the Devil from every side. It could not be a looking-glass, because the Green Man could see the back of the Devil's neck, which was creased with lines as deep as the bark of an old tree. He felt the back of his own neck and found them there too.

Coming round in front again he watched the Devil picking his pointed teeth with a twig, and saw that the Devil's eyes were his own eyes at certain times or phases of the moon. They were watchful and knowing and on the hypnotic side.

'We have not been introduced,' said the Green Man defensively.

'Oh, yes, we have,' said the Devil. 'We're reintroduced every day of our lives.'

'Your place is in hell,' said the Green Man. 'Each to his element.'

'My place is with you,' said the Devil. 'I'm in my element with you. Every minute of the day. You can't get away from me. Look at those mice and those mermaids.'

'I spared the mice and the mermaids,' said the Green Man.

'Only just,' said the Devil. 'And your daughters did the clearing-up. And what about your twelve sons?'

The Green Man fell silent. 'They are grown and flown,' he said. 'We are part of one another, therefore I have no guilt. I cannot go searching for them specifically. It isn't my destiny.'

'I have things to show you,' said the Devil. 'Perhaps you will accompany me to the moon and find your destiny?'

On the moon the two twins sat side by side upon a rock and looked down upon the beautiful blue planet, so small in the sky.

'Yours,' said the Devil.

'It's been said before,' said the Green Man. 'Are the conditions the same?'

'Yours,' said the Devil again. 'Here's a zap. Zap it.'

'No,' said the Green Man.

'Why not? The earth has never been good to you. Look how you've worked for it and loved it. Do you imagine that *places* love you back? A landscape doesn't hesitate to destroy you. Your fate has been predicted since humanity could predict. You are touched with death. You are strangled by the living green. Look at the old carvings of you in all those churches and ancient palaces. In the end you will vanish from the earth.'

'I keep away from carvings.'

'The Greeks and Romans made stone effigies of you and the Christians made copies. Over half the world there are images of you with vines growing like moustaches out of your nostrils. Then from your ears, and even your tongue. Sometimes they even grow from your eyeballs. Your beautiful face is the face of grief. You are born to die. It is eternal sorrow that stares through the leaves. Sad and bound is the Green Man.'

'There is Christ,' said the Green Man.

'Is there?' asked the Devil.

'Go on, zap them,' said the Devil. 'Zap them all, down there. You could.'

'There are my sons and daughters.'

'They don't care for you. You are nothing but a nuisance to them. You embarrass your sons. Your death would be welcome. You are a burden and a reproach.'

'They are part of me, my twelve sons. And my four daughters.'

'I'm part of you, too,' said the Devil. 'Let 'em go.'

The Green Man sat silent.

'The moon is clean and free,' said the Devil, 'untainted as yet by human wickedness. You with your green fingers could bring here the first new shoot, which would break into grasses and flowers, crops and forests. You could create a new world, perfect in God's sight. You yourself could be God. The wilderness would flower like no earthly paradise. Let the old world go.'

'I'd need the earth for back-up,' said the Green Man, weakening; and as he said it, some moss that had become caught in his hair — from a low branch of the apple tree — slid out of his leafy curls. A spider that had been living in the moss began a hasty thread from the curls to the moondust.

The Green Man watched the spider, which went tearing about here and there and bouncing up and down like a yo-yo. The Green Man held out his finger and tweaked the spider back, and for want of anywhere better flicked him up into his hair again. 'I cannot leave the greenwood,' he said.

'Almost everything else has,' said the Devil. 'And what you mean "greenwood"? D'you think you're Shakespeare or something?'

'I'm something,' said the Green Man.

'You're nothing at all,' said the Devil. 'You don't know who you are or what you are. All this about elements, you don't know your own. Nobody believes in you. You're kids' book stuff. They don't even call pubs after you any more. They change them to something from Walt Disney. The only ones who go on about you now are black-magic freaks who think you're something to do with me.'

'Not quite the only ones,' said the Green Man.

'Well – who else? The has-beens, the *hoi polloi*, the folk historians?'

'Sadie and Billy believed in me,' said the Green Man; 'and Patsy. And the corn chandler.'

'Who he?' asked the Devil, commonly.

'The water voles, the geese, the mice and the mermaids believe in me.'

'Oh, Christ!' said the Devil.

'Oh *what?*' said the Green Man.

The Devil stirred up the moon-dust with his finger, gently, so that the pressure didn't bounce him away. He seemed unenthusiastic about answering.

'D'you really think Christ cares about you?' he said at last. 'Think what a world you live in. Think what a wonder it could be and what he's allowed you to do with it. I tell you – forget him. Zap it. And him. Create the moon.'

'The moon is created.'

'Re-create it. Clothe it. Beautify it above the earth. Look at the potential, man. Look around you. A pure new architecture, rivers of silver, mountains of gold. After you've moved the space-trash of course.'

'I would spawn more.'

'Technology, man, technology. Enlightened clearances create a world of light. Get the straw from your hair. You spend whole days, whole years, scything the grass of an orchard nobody needs. You can get bags of apples half the price in the supermarket. And think of the space on the moon.

You could do it. With my help. All you have to do is believe in me.'

The Green Man tried now, seriously, to consider the Devil's rational good sense and to analyse what the earth and the moon really meant for him. He thought of the moon's calm light as it sailed above the branches of the orchard.

'It's not for me to change it,' he said.

'I'm disappointed in you,' said the Devil.

'I'm disappointed in *you*,' said the Green Man.

'But *why?*' asked the Devil with his sweet and loving smile.

'You're nothing but my shabby self,' said the Green Man. 'You're the dark side of my soul. You're *déjà vu.*'

The Devil then threw a rock at him and vanished and the Green Man in an instant was back in the orchard, under a Ribston Pippin. It was cold and raining and the fruits above his head looked ungrateful and sour. He found himself weeping and weak.

'I must sleep,' he said, 'here in the grass and the rain. When I wake perhaps I won't feel that it's been a defeat,' and he fell asleep in the grass that would be cut for hay on Saturday.

The spider walked out of his hair and spun a beautiful web across his tired eyes.

5 The Green Man Attends a Place of Worship

At harvest festival, like many farmers since its ancient institution and maybe only out of pagan habit, the Green Man sometimes goes to church. He goes to the early morning service, where there are few people. The church has always been lovingly decorated for harvest with flowers and vines and bines and trails of hops. There is bread, plaited or covered in cobnuts or marked into gold squares. There are no sheaves of corn these days, but tins of baked beans that are later taken to patients in hospital. Patients in hospital would be bewildered by sheaves. They are rather bewildered by baked beans and usually hand them over to their visitors. The visitors take them home and give them to their children when there has to be a contribution to the next school fête. The baked beans bought at the fête will be half-price and often come back to church for the next harvest festival. This is country life.

The Green Man is hard to discern among the hop bines and the baked beans in the church at harvest, but he is there if you look hard enough. He doesn't sit in the body of the church but tends to be up in the chancel, leaning against a pillar, peering through the decorations of harvest green and gold. Up above him on a corbel (*c.* 1220) his own effigy looks down. It is his own head, wrapped in vine leaves like a Greek dinner.

The Green Man's head, so beautiful, passionate, tormented, ardent, is being eaten up by oak leaves. He stares down at the living Green Man – who is listening gratefully to the Collect – and around the church which is his prison.

'I see myself everywhere,' says the living Green Man. 'First in the orchard,' he says, 'then on the moon. Good likenesses, though by no means exact. And I'm supposedly defunct. I am seldom noticed and when I am noticed everyone sees someone different: a tree, a scarecrow, a saint, a devil, or "That old guy on the farm; bit out of his element these days. Belongs to the past." They do not *peruse* my face. Sometimes they see me, sometimes they don't.'

'The fruits in their season,' intones the parson.

At the Gospel the Green Man turns to face the east end of the church, as has been his medieval way. This brings him to face his companions along the pew. It is the choir-stall pew of Transept Manor. Lord Transept and Lady Serena Transept, their cheerful cousin and the dog, stand in a row. All remain face forward in the aristocratic low-church way except the dog, who decides to face west and wag its tail at the Green Man. The cheerful cousin waves her handkerchief.

After the service Lady Serena Transept – tall, flat and slender as her ancestor who lies on top of a nearby tomb in wimple, camisole and long stone robe and who looks much like her except that Lady Serena has a long hooky nose. The ancestor had one too, but it was snipped off into a Cromwellian pocket – Lady Serena Transept turns to the Green Man and lays a long-fingered paw upon his Sunday-best green tweed arm. 'Come to breakfast,' she says.

So they all set forth to Transept Manor, Lady

Serena driving fast, through the swishing puddles of the mile-long avenue of dead elms. Lord Transept broods alongside and the cousin sits in the back humming hymns with the dog, who looks delighted. In the manor kitchen they drink tea and eat toast and the cousin selects the numbers for her lottery ticket and the dog lies ecstatic in the Green Man's lap. His lordship hangs in looming thought and Lady Serena strokes the back of the Green Man's hand.

'I never thought to meet you,' she said. 'I've looked up at you for years on the corbel.'

'Corbels and capitals, tympana and misericords,' says the Green Man: 'I'm all over the place yet nobody knows who I am. I am not all stone. I come to church for all the great festivals.'

'I know. I have seen you. So has my dog, but we never dared speak. I *feel* that I know you. I *know* that I know you. One knows a lot about the person one prays next to.'

'Marmalade,' says his lordship.

'Tootle-oo,' sings the cousin.

The dog sighs.

*

Outside, the rain has stopped and the drops on the bumpy diamonds of the window-panes turn the day to wet gold. Sunshine breaks across the cauliflower fields and lights a lanternyard of fruit trees, ten miles of hop-gardens, three needle spires and a stretch of Roman road on the horizon, where big lorries and tractor-vans roll along like toys.

The beams in the manor-house kitchen are made from oaks that may have dropped acorns on legionaries. Whoever decided to make a kitchen of them didn't bother to take off all the bark. There are bumps and sawn circles where branches have been trimmed off to be slung on to fires to roast oxen. The Green Man, surveying these timbers, reflects that there is nothing like them on the moon.

'Soon we shall *all* go to the moon,' says the jolly cousin.

His lordship says, 'These days I'm only able to put one foot in front of another.'

'Sometimes,' says his sister, 'you can't even do that.'

This scene in the manor kitchen the Green Man finds very comforting.

*

Lady Serena Transept walks with the Green Man part of the way home. He pushes his bicycle beside her along the avenue and she jumps the puddles like a giraffe (and she all of ninety), her spindle legs in thick, lace-patterned stockings.

'We are both old things,' she says: 'antiques. I and His Lordship and the Manor will soon be gone, and all our kind.'

'And, no doubt, I,' says the Green Man.

'Oh, I don't think so,' she says. 'I'd doubt that very seriously.'

6 The Green Man and the Loss-Adjuster's Woman

The Green Man is in the coppice, lean as a sapling, pausing with his axe, peering from his deep-set eyes through the silver branches. Who is this walking over the meadow towards his house? She disappears in a fold of the field where the house lies, and after some time she re-emerges and walks towards him. She has passed through his house, front door to back, for both stand open. Here she comes on her high heels, a snake, very thin, smoking a cigarette, which she throws away into the coppice. The Green Man is invisible in the bouquets of the ash clumps, his face dappled so that leaves seem to flicker and caress his cheeks, to sweep out of his eyebrows. *Who's this then?*

He watches carefully to make sure that the cigarette lies dead in the wood-chippings and the wood anemones. There is no glow.

She passes. She has a mean look. She wears town clothes, not warm enough, but quite respectable. She places her feet with care and they take her out of sight down to the great May trees and beyond; beyond the struggling elms and the whispering poplars, over the marsh. There she goes. Only a dot now. Over the marsh to the seaside.

Now, she is returning, and she passes through the coppice again and he sees her little watchful face. It is a closed face.

This time she side-steps his hidden house and soon he hears a motor starting up and driving away. The silence flows over the land again to be broken before long by the Green Man as he flings his axe against the sapling stalks in rhythmic chopping.

He works until nightfall and the wind has changed

and comes off the sea and he feels cold. He walks home thinking, I shall sleep indoors tonight. He has his axe over his shoulder and he whistles for the dog, but the dog doesn't come. He thinks of hot porridge and hot tea and maybe whisky before bed.

But there is no bed. There is no couch. There is no table. There is no chair. Gone is the small wooden-handled herb-chopper of ancient design, the barometer given him by the peripatetic academic folklorist, the hat that once belonged to Oliver Cromwell, willed him by a former Lord Transept. Gone are the books from the shelf, the lustre jug from the dresser, the gold comb with the seashells he bought at the door and has never liked. Gone is the black iron kettle on the chain and the iron griddle that hung from the rafters, the great court-cupboard mysteriously carved in Bremen and the jerry-pot of Meissen. Gone is the dog.

The Green Man walks in the east wind, calling for the dog. When at last he returns, he makes porridge, but not in the black pot, which needs both hands to be lifted to the fire and is lined with heavy silver; for that is gone.

There is a very old hearth-mat made of coloured

scraps of cloth from God knows which countries
and the Green Man wraps himself in this and sleeps
upon the floor.

In the morning, or perhaps several mornings later,
come some daughters lovely as lilies, early, and see
upon the floor this long roly-poly with head and
feet stuck out at either end and all the tufted patches
of old garment-scraps in between. There is the
scrap of an eighteenth-century smock, a nineteenth-
century bloomer, a snicket of liberty bodice with a
very small pearl button, the edge of a milkmaid's
petticoat and a glimpse of lavender silk from the
wedding dress worn by who knows who in the
Green Man's history, and all the women in it. His
green feet are sockless for his socks are gone.
His green hair floats about, for gone is his limpet-
covered comb. The Green Man in his bedding roll
is like a multi-coloured almond-slice in the window
of an eccentric pastry cook.

The dog, all burrs and sorrow, lies close beside
him on the floor.

Mugged! Dead! Police! Robbers!

Certainly robbers.

Retribution! Revenge!

But the Green Man sits up on an apple box and takes a mug of tea and picks burrs off the dog. The dog cannot stop shivering.

'Oh, we'll catch them all right,' says the policeman – a fishy, flashy fellow who has a past and doubtful friends. The Green Man has often heard him, sniffing about. 'We'll soon get the Loss-Adjuster in.' The Green Man is unaware of loss-adjusters and presumes them to be philosophers.

'You might also like a counsellor,' says the young policegirl, overweight and gorgeous. *I could counsel you*, her eyes say to the exotic animal-eyes of the Green Man, *after hours*.

'I have suffered no loss,' says the Green Man. 'I shall miss the little herb-chopper. And my socks, for they were knitted by someone close to me.'

'He enjoys frugality,' say the daughters, putting up a new bed and couch, setting stainless steel on the shelf. 'He's in his element away from plenty.'

The Green Man strokes his dog.

'Do you bring a charge then?' asks the policeman.

'Yes,' say the daughters.

'No,' says the Green Man. 'No charge, free for all.' Then, looking at the policeman, he says, 'I shall lose nothing.'

'I'd not count on that, Grandad. There was a big antiques fair at Newark last week and all will be gone to Holland in containers by now. You'll be insured of course? The Loss-Adjuster will see to you.'

The Green Man is not conversant with details of insurance policies.

Each to his element.

The policegirl can't keep away. She calls early and late, but after a time she does not find the Green Man at home. She shouts to him across the marshes, but there is no reply. He sleeps out in the coppices among the wood anemones and relies on Indian take-aways from the next-door farmers, old and young Mr Jackson. 'Hello?' she calls. 'Are you there? It's me, Pearly.' She thinks of him all the time. She will never forget him. She is never to meet such another. She wanders, dreaming through the coppice, in her black police shoes, over the dykes.

The long wet grasses brush her strapping legs. She leaves a daring note one day on the new plastic table in the kitchen, with a box of chocolates and a dozen pairs of socks marked 'Nylon Rich'.

The Green Man doesn't understand the note and feeds the chocolates to the dog. The socks revolt him.

One day, comes the first woman again on her high heels over the meadow. She looks to left and right and smokes her cigarette and when she gets to the coppice this time her eyes have become accustomed to the light and she sees the Green Man standing there. She makes to throw away the cigarette but then rubs it out on the sole of her shoe and puts it in her pocket. 'Hi,' she says. She seems uneasy. He does not speak.

'My partner is the Loss-Adjuster and he's down in the car, waiting.'

'I have not suffered loss.'

'You have been victimised. By someone who knew everything about you.'

'*Everything* about me?'

She blushes, and pretends to be bored. 'He's come to make an assessment.'

'An assessment of me?'

'He's the policeman's twin brother.'

'Ah.'

There falls a silence until the Green Man walks across to her in the whispering wood-chips that scent the air among the wood anemones. There are bluebells now, too. Such bluebells! Smoke on summer eves. The scent of bluebells lasts for one week only.

The Green Man carries his glistening axe over his shoulder and comes close to the woman and looks down, down into her troubled eyes. He takes the axe from his shoulder with both his hands and holds it high.

She cannot move.

Then he places it in the woman's stained hands with their chipped red nails and says, 'Take this, too.'

She throws it to the ground and runs away, stumbling back across the meadow.

As she passes the house the dog shoots out and goes for her heels, snap, snap. He remembers her.

He remembers, too, the Loss-Adjuster who is sitting in the car.

The Loss-Adjuster is not keen to get out of the car.

'He won't take money,' says the woman, falling into the seat beside him, the dog raising merry hell.

'Why you all over 'im? Let 'im be,' says the Loss-Adjuster. He smells of guilt and sweating fear that glistens on his cheeks.

'He could get us caught,' squeals his woman.

'Get on, 'e's a lunatic.'

'I don't know what he is,' she says, crying.

The Green Man stands now on a rise behind the invisible house, watching them. The evening sun flames on his woodland limbs, his axe gleams, his hair blows green in the wind.

''e's from the 'Sixties. 'e was a drug-addict,' says the Loss-Adjuster. 'There's stories about 'im. Forget it, can't you?'

'We've got to get it all back to him. He's bad news.'

''e doesn't want it,' says the Loss-Adjuster. 'Pearl said. She's gone soft on 'im.'

Then the Loss-Adjuster's woman is filled with a

raving jealousy and she tries to get out of the car.
'I must go back and be with the Green Man,' she
cries, and the sweaty Loss-Adjuster socks her and
starts the car and tries to drive it away down the
lanes where sometimes farm machinery passes along,
each machine the length and height of a street of
houses. One of these in a moment meets the Loss-
Adjuster and his Moll on the corner of a flax field,
oh, such a colour, more gentle, more shadowy blue
even than bluebells, blue as a tender morning sky
and now splattered all over with scarlet.

The policegirl is back soon to try to counsel the
Green Man all over again in his double tragedy, but
he looks over her head, far, far away.

'Don't you care about *anything*?' she weeps then.
'*Why* can't you need comfort?'

So he takes her home for a time, then makes her
some tea in a tin mug and sends her away with the
multi-coloured rug of paduasoy and glazed linen
and sprig-muslin snips, of velveteen and taffeta and
tussore, a shred or two of hair shirt but much *point
d'ésprit* and threadwork and black work and bead
work and hedebo, and rich lazy-daisy and faggoting

and Venetian *toile cirée*. The old rug is backed with flour bags, and she keeps it all her life.

7 The Green Man Meets his Maker

The gold-and-rose-coloured autumn is gone and in November come the wind and the rain and the Green Man's twelve sons in a minibus. He sees it from his kitchen window, and closes his eyes. In they all stream. 'What a disgrace! You look ill! You look haggard! Who looks after you? Where are our sisters?'

'They are on a short holiday in the south of France.'

'Lucky for some. *They* don't work like we do. *We* can't afford holidays in the south of France. And how stupid, too, the south of France at this time of the year. You are living so poor. You need paint and wallpaper. Your roof is full of holes. You will shame us in the neighbourhood. What's for dinner?'

'I'm afraid I no longer eat dinner. I no longer need it.'

'You are undernourished. You have leaves in your hair. Let me get on the blower for supplies, carpenters, painters. Amenities.'

'Amenities?'

'The electricity board, the telephone centre, the television and video shop.'

'And to the Authorities,' says the eldest son. 'There are excellent homes for the elderly.'

'I am not elderly,' says the Green Man, 'I am the Green Man.'

'Hello? Hello? Yes, he needs help. He is alone. Practically *unfurnished*. We think it has affected his mind.'

'Out!' shouts the Green Man. 'The lot of you. Back to your element,' and he picks up a flail that leans by the back door and begins to strike out about him, clubbing some of them on the head.

They scatter in their sharp suits, clutching their mobile phones. All except the youngest, who turns back and says, 'Sorry it's been so long, Dad. It's easy to forget the passage of time.'

'I've stood so long in the passage of time,' says the Green Man; 'it is my home sweet home.'

'Can you manage?' asks the youngest son (and

another one, possibly Number Six, who's not as bad as most of the rest, peeps round the door and fingers his club tie). 'Have you enough money?'

'Money has never been a trouble to me.'

'Have you enough food?' and he lifts the lid of the flour crock and sees the drum marked MOUSE POISON.

'Mouse poison in the flour crock!' cries the eldest awful son with his blow-dried hair, coming back into the kitchen. '*That* does it. Not fit to live alone.' He picks up the drum and makes off with it to the minibus, where the rest of the brothers are glaring through the windows.

'We'll take it back to the corn chandler and get him to send you some bread,' says the kindly, though feeble, youngest son.

'He doesn't deliver.'

'I'm sure that he would.'

'Goodbye,' says the Green Man, stern as Ulysses.

He watches the minibus depart, driven erratically and bad-temperedly by the eldest son. The youngest son waves from the window.

'Thank God,' says the Green Man and lies down on

his old couch and listens to the silence. After a time, edging into the silence, a wind begins to blow across his fields, a soft wind but whispering of winter. The Green Man sleeps.

Then the Green Man has a dream. He dreams that the wind has strengthened and is tearing at his house in the fold of the fields and that he hears branches and sheds come crashing down. He dreams that he goes to fasten the clattery window in the kitchen, and there outside, beneath a leafless tree in the apple orchard, stands a figure who looks as if he owns the place. Before shutting the window the Green Man shouts, 'Get off my land.'

Then he wraps himself in an extra sack and goes outdoors.

'What do you think you're doing in my orchard?' he cries.

'I'm standing on next year's daffodils,' says the man.

The man's clothes do not blow in the mighty wind. Otherwise his figure is similar to that of the Green Man. He is tall and lean and wears something much like a sack. This time it is certainly not the Devil.

The Green Man thinks again, *I must be seeing*

through a looking-glass, and he walks right round the man. The man's hair is longer than the Devil's so that the Green Man cannot examine the lines in his neck. Nevertheless he thinks, *This is myself.* But when he has come full circle and looks into the man's eyes, he sees that the man is Christ.

The Green Man falls to his knees, but Christ raises him up.

'Your troubles are over,' says Christ.

'You mean I am about to die?'

'I mean that there is no Death,' says Christ. 'Today you will be with me in paradise.'

'But I'm the Green Man. The earth is my element. This is my tragedy. You know this. I am bound and tied. The very meaning of me is not known. You do not include me.'

Christ said, 'The Green Man is no enemy of Christ.'

The Green Man woke from his dreams and the wind was not the soft wind to which he had fallen asleep: it was shrieking and howling as it had done in the dream orchard.

It was daylight, and he went to fasten the clattering window, outside which nobody stood under the trees.

'I shall eat some bread,' said the Green Man. He felt very tired. 'And I shall drink some water.' Then he remembered that the flour crock was empty. The water down in the field dyke felt far away.

So he thought, *I'll rest a bit longer*, and lay down again on the couch. Soon he began to feel peaceful. 'I shall wait here for Death,' he said. 'Here it comes.'

Soon, far away down the lanes, he heard the sound of Death approaching. It was a great black Yamaha. Its rider sat astride it, a black figure in black visor and black armour. Black gauntlets grasped the black handlebars. The noise of the great bike seemed to silence the wind.

'It is here,' said the Green Man as the motorbike shuddered, surged and stopped at his gate. He walked to his front door and opened it on the black day.

Death pushed his steed right to the Green Man's threshold. Fastened to its flank was a box with a lid and a strap.

Too small for a coffin, thought the Green Man. *Maybe it's for my ashes.*

'Can I bring it round the back,' asked Death, 'in case it gets nicked at-all?'

'*Nicked?*' said the Green Man. 'I don't think Nick's here any more. He's gone. You needn't fear him. This is a good place now, and I am ready to die.'

'To *die?*' said Death. 'Oh, come on now!' And Death removed the black helmet and unzipped the black leathers.

Out stepped a girl like a spring flower, and all of sixteen. 'I am the corn chandler's daughter,' she said, 'and I've brought you some bread.'

They looked, and they loved.

'It is a miracle!' said the corn chandler's daughter in the Green Man's arms.

'It is heaven!' she said on the Green Man's couch.

'And it is impossible,' she said in the Green Man's bed, 'for I am to be married on Saturday to Jackson, your next-door farmer.'

And she was. The bells of the steeple rang out for her (a quiet bride) on the Saturday afternoon.

Earlier that week, one bright and frosty day, they had begun to toll for many hours, a peal for each year of the Green Man's life. The mice heard the knell in the pockets of the old mackintosh on the back of his kitchen door. The water voles and the swans heard it in the dykes. The geese heard it, flying south. The seagulls heard it. (They think they are nobody's fool and guessed what it was.) Sadie and Billy and Patsy and their grandchildren heard it on the farms around and said, 'How endlessly it tolls. It must be for the Green Man.'

Deep in the winter sea the mermaids heard it, and didn't much care. The twelve sons didn't hear it because they were all at foreign conferences, but the four daughters on a cold beach in France heard it in their hearts. A shiver passed among them and they looked at one another sadly. Lady Serena Transept and her cousin and the dog heard it and went specially to sit in the Manor pew to listen; and occasionally the dog howled. Above them the head on the stone corbel peered through its leaves to watch the ringers and Lord Transept, who had asked particularly to toll the final knell.

*

In the high street of the market town the corn chandler heard it and he smiled. He knew the future, being a reading man.

And was unsurprised, therefore, some years later, a green-eyed grandson on his knee, to hear that somebody going through the lanes towards the tip to dump his Christmas tree had seen a shadow standing in the fields.

Acknowledgements

Some of the stories in this collection first appeared in the following publications: 'Missing the Midnight' © 1995 Jane Gardam, *The Oldie*, 1995; 'The Zoo at Christmas' © 1995 Jane Gardam, *The Spectator*, 1995; 'Old Filth' © 1996 Jane Gardam, *The Oldie*, 1996; 'Miss Mistletoe' © 1994 Jane Gardam, *The Oldie*, 1994; 'Grace' © 1994 Jane Gardam, *Daily Telegraph*, 1994; 'Light' © 1994 Jane Gardam, *Marie Claire*, 1994; 'The Girl with the Golden Ears' © 1996 Jane Gardam, *Raconteur*, 1996; 'The Boy who Turned into a Bike' © 1995 Jane Gardam, *You* magazine, 1995; 'The Pillow Goose' © 1995 Jane Gardam, *Telling Stories 4*, Sceptre, 1995.

'Soul Mates' was commissioned by the BBC and has been broadcast on Radio 4.